DOCTOR GREGORY ON CALL

Kitty and her brother had to leave home when their father told them he was about to marry again and she found a new life in a small flat. Before long, however, Kitty's well-paid secretarial job is lost when the firm goes into receivership. Having struck up a friendship with Patricia Mason, a physiotherapist who lives next door, Kitty is offered a job at the hospital, as a counter hand in the doctor's cafeteria. After meeting Doctor Gregory, Kitty finds her life changes considerably, and she is not at all sure that it is for the better ...

DOCTOR GREGORY ON CALL

Doctor Gregory On Call

by
Grace M. Phipps

Dales Large Print Books
Long Preston, North Yorkshire,
England.

British Library Cataloguing in Publication Data.

Phipps, Grace M.
  Doctor Gregory on call.

  A catalogue record for this book is
  available from the British Library

  ISBN 1-85389-937-2 pbk

First published in Great Britain by Robert Hale Ltd., 1980

Copyright © 1980 by Grace M. Phipps

Cover photography by arrangement with RJB Photo Library

The moral right of the author has been asserted

Published in Large Print 1999 by arrangement with Robert
Hale Ltd.

Dales Large Print is an imprint of
Library Magna Books Ltd.
Printed and bound in Great Britain by
T.J. International Ltd., Cornwall, PL28 8RW.

AUTHOR'S NOTE

All the characters in this book, and also the hospital cafeteria have no existence outside the imagination of the author.

ONE

The three members of the Willet household, father, son and daughter were about to leave the house for their respective jobs when Herbert Willet made an announcement.

'Just a minute,' he said. 'I've something to tell you.'

Kitty and Richard stopped and regarded their father in some irritation.

'I'll be late,' said Kitty. 'Mr. Chester has a board meeting this morning and I'm expected to have all the data ready by ten.'

'And I've got plenty on my plate, too,' said Richard, 'so make it snappy.'

'Very well. Snappy it shall be.' Herbert Willet cleared his throat and said without more ado, 'I'm getting married in two weeks' time and I'd like you both to find board elsewhere.'

'Board!' said Richard. 'But this is our home. We pull our weight with the housekeeping. How can you turn us out?'

Kitty said, 'Married! I don't believe it. Why, you're over fifty.'

Herbert became somewhat belligerent. 'Now, listen here. A man's not old at fifty and I've been very lonely these last two years since your mother died.'

'But *we've* been here,' said Kitty. 'It was our loss, too, you know.'

'You'll both be getting married yourselves before too long, no doubt. And remember this. I'm not asking your permission. I'm telling you.'

'Who is she?' asked Richard.

'She is a very upright and honourable woman.'

'Not too young, I hope,' said Richard.

'She is Miss Myra Thacker and she's a school teacher—teaches commercial at St.

10

Elmo's private college.'

'Miss Thacker! I know her,' said Kitty. 'She took a relieving job at High school for a few weeks when I was there. She was so strict we nearly all went berserk. Do you realise what you're letting yourself in for, Dad? She berated us for our sins every single day.'

'You probably deserved it,' said Mr. Willet. 'Personally, I find Myra a very pleasant and amiable person.'

'You'll find out. And don't say I didn't warn you.' Kitty looked at her watch. 'I'm going to be late. Must dash.'

Richard said, 'I'll run you to your office.'

'It's out of your way,' said Kitty.

'I'll make haste—with caution.' Richard took her arm and hustled her out of the house.

Squashed beside her brother in the small runabout, Kitty said, 'What a bombshell to drop on us—and this early in the morning. Turfed out of our home. We're orphans,

Rich. At least it feels like it even though we do have a father and a step-mother looming.'

'To tell you the truth,' said Richard, 'I was contemplating leaving home. Some chaps I know rent a house and they're looking for another flat-mate as one of their number is leaving. Nevertheless, I resent being *told* to go.'

'Same here. I'm glad you've somewhere to go to. I think I'll look around for a small flat. It might be quite nice to be independent. It had crossed my mind that it would be fun to leave home, but I was staying from a sense of duty, not liking to leave you and Dad to manage for yourselves.'

They had reached the building where Kitty worked and she said goodbye to Richard and ran up the stairs to the office of Chester and Wearman, a large firm of clothing manufacturers.

Kitty had a well-paid position as secretary to Mr. Chester, the manager. She was efficient and reliable, and Mr. Chester had come to depend on her ability to deal in a tactful way with any complaints from buyers in the retail trade.

The morning passed quickly, as board meeting day was a busy one for Kitty and her own problems, of necessity, had to be pushed into the background of her mind. But at lunchtime, the fact that she had to find somewhere to live—in double-quick time—hit her in full force.

She hurried to the canteen, swallowed a cup of tea and a sandwich as speedily as she could and then went into the streets hoping to find a land agent who ran a renting department.

She was lucky with her first one. A polite young man listened to her requirements, went through his books, then wrote her a very short list.

'These are fairly handy to town,' he told her. 'You might even have time to look at a couple in your dinner hour.'

Kitty scanned the list, thanked the agent,

and then made haste to the one that sounded attractive—One-bedroom flat in Tamara Place, quiet surroundings, near bus route, five minutes from city. She caught a bus and found the house, staring up at the old, two-storied brick residence which had been converted into flats, and deciding that it might be just the thing.

A row of doorbells was in a panel outside, and Kitty rang No. 2, then proceeded up the stairs. When she knocked, the door of the flat was opened by a young woman of about twenty-five.

Kitty said, 'Are you Miss Kelly? I've come about the flat.' She held out the agent's card.

'Oh, yes. Come inside,' said Miss Kelly. 'I'm in a bit of a mess—in the middle of packing as you can see. I'm moving out tomorrow. I've landed a job in Auckland. My fiancé lives up there and we'll be getting married shortly. This isn't a bad flat, convenient to town and all mod. cons. I'll show you round.'

The entrance hall which was stacked with suitcases, had three doors. One opened on to a living-room carpeted in moss green. Off this was a minute kitchen, but it housed a refrigerator, washing machine, one wall of cupboards and a stainless steel sink and bench.

'Everything's convenient,' said Miss Kelly. 'You can stand in the centre and just about reach everything. The bathroom is through that other door off the hall.'

Back in the living-room, Kitty said, 'Does any furniture go with the place?'

'That divan does, also the two chairs and the sideboard, which is handy for extra crockery. Now come and see the bedroom. It's small, but not too bad.'

'Oh, I like it,' said Kitty, noting the built-in wardrobe and dressing-table, the moss green carpet and the plain, cream walls.'

'You won't get any better for the price.'

'How much is it?'

'Thirty-five dollars a week. I'd advise

you to take it. It's reasonable, as flats go, especially this near the city.'

'What are the other tenants like?'

'Well, they come and go. Mostly, they're fairly quiet, but of course, there's the odd occasion when someone throws a party, and then there's not much sleep for the rest of us.'

'I've another one to look at,' said Kitty, glancing at her watch. 'It's not far from here. I'll just have time if I hurry.'

'Rightio. I hope you're soon satisfied. Oh, by the way, if you take this flat, prevail on the landlord to fix the stove. One of the electric elements on the top has gone.'

'I'll do that.'

The next flat was two blocks away, and Kitty was there in ten minutes. This was one of a row of modern flats. An elderly woman answered the door. Kitty produced the agent's card, and the woman said with some asperity, 'I don't *have* to let people through here. Why can't they leave me in peace until I move out?'

'If it's not convenient,' said Kitty, backing off, 'I shall quite understand.'

The old woman opened the door wider. 'Oh, well, now as you're here, you might as well come in and take a look. I'm going into a home next week as I'm getting past looking after myself. Most of my furniture will go to the auction rooms, but I would consider selling it to whoever wants to move in here, that is, if I got a fair price.'

The front door opened straight into a living-cum-dining room. It was cluttered with sagging chairs and an equally drab sofa. Three small tables were crowded with photographs and an old clock ticked wheezily on a wall bracket.

The kitchen was so small that only one person could squeeze into it. The bedroom was a reasonable size and contained a large walk-in wardrobe. A bathroom with shower and basin opened off.

'They've just put the rent up,' confided

the old lady. 'It's thirty-five dollars a week, which takes about half my pension, so it don't give me much to live on, what with the price of electricity and everything going up as well.'

'Well, thanks for letting me see it,' said Kitty, deciding at once that the other place was far better value.

She arrived back at the office five minutes late and had no sooner seated herself at her desk when Mr. Chester rang for her.

She picked up her notebook and pencil and went into his office.

Mr. Chester said, 'I imagine you've guessed by what was said at the board meeting that we've had a very poor year.'

'I know that orders have been falling off for some time.'

'We've lost most of the Australian market,' said Mr. Chester, 'and, consequently, we will have to cut down on some of the staff, which, of course, we don't like doing.'

Kitty, whose mind had been half on her accommodation problems, became immediately alert. Was Mr. Chester trying to break it gently that he was going to sack *her*? She waited in trepidation for him to go on.

Mr. Chester, a well-knit man of fifty-five, ran his hands through his hair, a gesture he used only when worried.

'I've been consulting the factory manager —Sims—during the lunch hour, and we've made out a list between us. I want you to type dismissal notices to be enclosed with their wages this week. I'll leave it to you to work out something tactful. You'll know what to say—that we've appreciated their cooperation with the firm and regret that, owing to circumstances beyond our control, they've been made redundant. They'll all get good references, of course.' He held out a piece of paper. 'Here's the list of names.'

Kitty went back to her small private office and regarded the list with dismay.

There were at least thirty names on it. Most of the men were married with children. What a rotten thing to have to do! Tell them they were redundant! It was like saying, 'Go and throw yourselves on the scrap-heap.' She was glad she wouldn't be the one to hand out the envelopes. That duty would fall to Mr. Elderton, the accountant.

Kitty was hard at work when the junior typist from the large office came in with a cup of tea at three o'clock. She put it on the desk beside Kitty, glancing as she did so, at the growing pile of letters on the table.

'What a lot of letters,' said the girl, Josie. 'Want me to do the envelopes?'

Kitty hastily turned the top letter of the pile over before Josie could read it. 'No, I've nearly finished. I've heaps of time to do the envelopes, thanks, Josie.'

Kitty had almost sweated blood over the first draft of the letter, but no matter how she tried to gild the pill, there was no way of softening the bitter taste of dismissal.

When she'd finished her unwelcome task, she took the letters in to Mr. Chester for his signature. He read the top copy.

'Excellent,' he said, giving her a feeble smile.

'It's still the sack,' said Kitty.

'It hurts me to do it,' said Mr. Chester gruffly. 'Apart from the odd rebel, they've been loyal employees, but we can't keep running at a loss.'

'What about the machines lying idle?' asked Kitty.

'Some will have to be sold. We're going to try and whip up local trade and hope things will pick up later in the year. It's not only Chester and Wearman, you know. Things have been tough for a number of firms.'

'Yes, I know,' said Kitty. 'There's news in the papers every day of some firm or another having to either close or cut down staff.'

She left the office that afternoon with

a heavy heart. As she passed the land agent's office, she saw that it was still open and decided to clinch the deal for the Tamara Place flat before someone else snapped it up.

She came out with a contract in her purse. It was for only three months and she had had to pay a month's rent in advance. Luckily she had just enough money on her for that. Now she would be able to move in next weekend.

She arrived home at five-thirty and, as she bustled around the kitchen preparing a meal, Richard came in looking pleased with himself.

'I'm fixed up for sharing a house,' he said.

'Oh, good,' said Kitty. 'When are you moving in?'

'Saturday. How about you? I suppose you haven't had time to look at flats.'

'Yes, I have. I've signed up for a three months' lease of one. It's in Tamara Place, and it's very nice. It's furnished, too.'

'How big is it?'

'One bedroom, a living-room, kitchen and bath.'

'When can you have it?'

'Saturday. So we'll both be moving out of here on the same day. Oh, goodness, that will leave Dad on his own for a couple of weeks. I hadn't thought of that.'

'Don't waste your pity on him, Kit. He had no qualms in giving us the push.' Richard looked disgruntled for a moment, his father's request for them to move out still rankling.

'Well, I suppose the redoubtable Myra can have him around for meals wherever she lives. Being a school teacher, she would be home early.'

Kitty was just making the gravy for the chops when Herbert Willet came in the back door.

'Something smells good,' he said.

'It's only chops,' said Kitty. 'Can your intended cook?'

'I've no idea,' said Herbert, 'but I guess

she can. She's been living with her mother, but the old lady died several months ago, and Myra has sold their home.'

'However did you meet her?' asked Kitty as she prodded the simmering potatoes with a fork to see if they were done.

'She came to my office about her mother's insurance. We met several times in the office, and when the insurance was fixed up, she kept calling in for my advice about what to do with the house. Then I took her out for dinner and, well ... she's a very attractive woman and she needs a man to look after her. She's finding life rather lonely since her mother died.'

Kitty began mashing the potatoes. 'Richard and I have some news for you, Dad. You'll be pleased to know we're both fixed up for flats. Rich is sharing with some chaps and I have found a very nice flat of my own.'

'Oh! When are you going?'

'Saturday. Both of us,' said Kitty.

'So soon? But Myra and I aren't getting

married for a week or two. You can't leave me here on my own.'

Richard, wandering in from the living-room, and hearing this last remark, said, 'We can and all. We're not asking if we can leave. We're telling you.'

Mr. Willet's face dropped, and Kitty said placatingly, 'Don't mind Richard, Dad. He's peeved at the way you told us both to go this morning.'

Herbert sank into a kitchen chair. 'Look, I'm sorry kids. I guess you both got a shock that your old man could contemplate marriage for a second time, and I guess I may have sounded a trifle harsh, but there is no need to rush right off in less than a week.'

'Well, it's done now,' said Richard. 'We're doing what *you* want, even if it's not exactly *when* you want it.'

Kitty said, 'I'll cook you a meal at my flat now and again, and you can manage until you get married by having hot lunches in town.'

Herbert looked downcast for a moment, as if the thought of the coming upheaval was more than he had bargained for. Then he said philosophically, 'Well, as Rich says, what's done is done. Where's the evening paper?'

'On your chair in the living-room,' said Kitty. 'Dinner will be on the table in a couple of seconds.'

When he'd gone, Richard threw out his hands in mingled dismay and amusement. 'I do believe he's beginning to think he's bitten off more than he can chew.'

TWO

Saturday morning arrived with lightning speed. Kitty had packed all her clothes, but there were bits and pieces of china and some pictures that belonged to her.

Richard had no problems. He threw his clothes, his athletic cups and his tennis racket into one big suitcase and odds and ends into a haversack, and was finished in under an hour.

Herbert wandered around watching their activities, his face expressing bewilderment and loss.

'The house is going to look bare without all your clutter,' he said.

'Not to worry,' said Richard. 'Myra will soon fill it up with her stuff. I guess she has plenty.'

'She's not keeping much,' said Herbert.

'The house is going to be auctioned, and the furniture with it.'

'She'll have personal things,' said Kitty, 'and as we'll soon be gone, she can start bringing her stuff right away.'

Richard went off with his gear in the car and then returned to take Kitty's cases. Kitty, meanwhile, had made a stew for Herbert, telling him it should last for a couple of days.

'You could come back to lunch and share it with me,' Herbert said tentatively.

'Dad, I need to spend the day getting my flat straight,' replied Kitty. 'Why don't you ring Myra and ask her over?'

'I could do that, I suppose, but she did tell me she has a very busy day planned, sorting out all her mother's belongings.'

Kitty felt a pang of guilt that she was leaving her father all by himself. She put an arm around his neck. 'Cheer up, Dad. You've a lot to look forward to. Why not do some gardening? The edges could do with a trim.'

'Yes, I suppose I'd better have it looking neat for when Myra comes.'

Once in the flat, Kitty had no time to worry further about her father. Richard had dumped her belongings in the middle of the living-room and had said, 'You'll be all right now?' and had gone off, eager to settle in with his male pals.

Kitty plunged into the job of making order out of chaos, first of all unpacking and hanging up her clothes in the wardrobe, and then making the bed and putting kitchen things away.

She was feeling completely exhausted and famished when there was a knock on the door. She saw a tall, well-built girl with a beaming smile standing there, a covered plate in her hand.

'I'm in the next flat,' she said. 'I thought you might be ready for some sustenance.'

'Am I ever!' said Kitty. 'Come in.'

'It's just a pizza pie—home made and full of nourishment, and you'd better eat it while it's hot. Where's your cutlery?'

'In that drawer under the sink,' said Kitty.

'Well, you have a wash and I'll set it up for you.' When Kitty returned from the bathroom, her hands washed and her face clean and shining, the table was set for one, the pizza was on a plate looking most attractive with a surround of baked tomatoes and some small, new potatoes with a sprig of parsley.

'Oh, that looks delicious,' exclaimed Kitty. 'Won't you share it with me? There's surely enough for two.'

'Thanks, but mine's in the oven. By the way, my name's Patricia Matson. Everyone calls me Pat.'

'I'm Kitty Willet. I'm awfully pleased to meet you.'

'And me, you. I'll see you later, Kitty.'

Kitty ate the meal with utmost enjoyment, heightened by the knowledge that she had a friendly, likeable neighbour.

After the meal, she washed the plate and went to Pat's flat to return it. When Pat opened the door, she invited Kitty inside.

'Come and have a wee chat while I finish my ironing,' she said.

Pat's flat was similar to Kitty's. The ironing board, which let down from the wall, had a bundle of smalls on it, and Kitty realised with a jolt that she didn't possess an iron. Luckily most of her garments were of the drip-dry variety, so the purchase of an iron wasn't urgent.

As if reading her thoughts, Pat said, 'If you haven't an iron, you can have a loan of mine any time. Now, tell me, what sort of a job do you have?'

'I'm secretary at Chester and Wearman's. What do you do?'

'I'm a physio-therapist at the public hospital. It's hard work, but I love it.' She flexed the muscles in her arms. 'As you can see, I'm well equipped for it.'

'It must be interesting.'

'It sure is. I get to meet all sorts.'

Kitty rose. 'I must be going. And thanks again for the lovely meal. I was feeling a bit lost when you knocked on my door.'

By five o'clock, Kitty was practically straight. She walked around the flat with a proprietary air, feeling complacent that she had managed to find herself a new home so quickly. The sight of her own possessions gave her a sense of belonging. If she had insisted on staying at home, Myra's presence would have made her feel odd-one-out, and she couldn't have borne that.

There were still lots of things she needed to buy to give the place a real lift, but it would be fun shopping for them.

She boiled an egg and made a couple of slices of toast for her tea, sitting comfortably on the divan with the tray on her knee. She had just finished when there was a knock on the door.

She opened it, thinking it would be Pat, but a young man stood there almost hidden by a large bunch of flowers.

'I'm Neil Woodward,' he said, 'and I live in the annex just outside the back door. Pat told me you'd just moved in, so I've brought you these flowers.'

'They're lovely,' said Kitty, not knowing whether or not to invite this cheerful, red-haired young man inside.

He said, 'I didn't *buy* them. My mum brought them in from the country, together with loads of food. She thinks her baby son can't manage on his own in the big city, so hence these periodical visits laden with goodies. She's a pet, actually, but you'll do me a favour if you'll accept these flowers. I've got some chaps coming round tonight and one of them gets hay fever if he's within cooee of a sweet pea.'

'Thank you very much. They're just what I need to make this place feel like home.'

'You're welcome,' said Neil, thrusting the flowers into Kitty's arms. 'Now I must be off.'

When he'd gone, Kitty, not having brought a vase with her, took down a couple of tumblers and arranged the sweet peas and some mignonette in one of them, and the taller flowers in the other, enjoying their fragrance as she placed one container on the mantelpiece and the other on a small table.

There was a phone in the living-room and Kitty, having obtained Richard's phone number before she had left him, rang her brother to see how he was faring.

When Richard answered, she said, 'How are you getting on, Rich?'

'Splendidly, so far. I'd like to see you fairly soon, though, Kitty. The chaps here take turns with the evening meal, and I haven't had much experience at cooking. I'd like a few basic hints so that I don't make too big a fool of myself.'

'Could you come round right now? I'm practically settled in.'

'In about half an hour. We've just finished our meal and, as I didn't do any of the preparation, I'm scheduled for the dishes.'

'See you then,' said Kitty, glad of the

prospect of some company. She had no television set, and the battery in her transistor radio was running low. She must remember to buy a new one.

Richard arrived about seven-thirty and surveyed the flat appraisingly.

'Very nice. I say, where'd you get the flowers?'

'From a neighbour downstairs—one Neil Woodward.'

'He's pretty quick off the mark, isn't he?'

'You could say that,' said Kitty, 'but it's not as romantic as it appears. His mother brought in the flowers from the country, and as Neil is expecting a caller who gets hay fever, it turns out I'm just a dumping ground for the sweet peas.'

'What's he like?'

'Pleasant. Homely, with red hair— nothing to go wild over. I have another good neighbour, too. Patricia Matson. She brought me a tray of lunch. It seems I've fallen on my feet. I had heard you could live in a block of flats and never know who your neighbours were, and here I've met two already.'

'I'm glad to hear that. I was a bit worried about you. Now, tell me how to cook chops and steak. I've got to do one or the other tomorrow.'

When Kitty had written down the basic points, Richard said, 'Thanks, pal. I'm sorry I can't stay. Des and Andy are going to the motor-car racing. Would you care to come along? You could be ready if you hurry.'

Kitty considered the invitation. 'I think not, Dickie. It's been a long day and I'd like an early night.'

'Rightio. Some other time, perhaps. We must keep in touch, Kitty. I feel as if you're the only family I've got now, what with Dad setting himself up with a wife and making us feel unwanted.'

'We might be glad he's got someone to look after him later on when we get married ourselves.'

'Hey, have you someone in view that I don't know about?'

Kitty laughed. 'You know me—the fussy one? I've yet to meet the man of my dreams, and until I do ...'

'Well, don't let yourself become too wedded to that job of yours.'

'There's plenty of time,' said Kitty. 'And I'd advise *you* not to tie yourself down too soon, young Richard.'

'Hark to my sister who is one whole year younger than I am. Well, I must be off. Can't keep the chaps waiting.' Richard gave her an affectionate whack on her rear and went off, whistling.

Kitty decided to have a bath, then go to bed and read. Her legs ached and she felt exceedingly sleepy. The bath was a small, narrow one with an overhead shower which dripped maddeningly, but a washer should fix that, and a daily, morning shower would be handy and quick. But tonight, a long soak in a hot bath was what she needed, and she lingered longer than she meant to in the warm, soothing water.

She had no sooner climbed into bed and opened her book when she heard sounds of arrival at Neil Woodward's flat. Neil's voice was loud and welcoming and his friends had correspondingly hearty voices. Then Neil's door shut and all was quiet.

Kitty, her eyelids drooping, put down her book and, although it was only nine o'clock, turned out the light.

It seemed she had been asleep for only five minutes when she was woken by a cacophony of sound—the clash of cymbals, electric guitars and drums. Pop music, all erupting from Neil Woodward's flat.

Surely they wouldn't keep *that* up for long. But they did. At eleven p.m. they were still going strong, and Kitty thought she might as well stay awake and try to enjoy it instead of fuming. But the same stanza was repeated over and over again until Kitty, in desperation, got up and made herself a cup of coffee and hunted around for some cotton wool to plug in her ears. Why had she left her nice, quiet home?

The cotton wool helped a little and, blessedly, at midnight, the noise suddenly ceased. Well, she wouldn't complain to Neil about it. Probably it was only on a Saturday night that he had his friends around, and some Saturdays he might even go to the other men's places. Anyway, he seemed a reasonable young man who wouldn't go out of his way to annoy neighbours. And he *had* given her those lovely flowers.

On Sunday morning Kitty got up late, glad that it wasn't a working day. There was a fairly large yard at the back of the flats, and this was taken up with a row of garages and a couple of whirligig clotheslines.

Kitty, from her upstairs window, saw Patricia Matson hanging out some washing, and called down to her, 'Would you like some coffee? That is, if you're not too busy.'

'Love some,' called back Patricia. 'Give me five minutes and I'll be there.'

Over the coffee and biscuits, Patricia said, 'I hope Neil Woodward's racket didn't keep you awake last night.'

'Well, it did. Does he have these friends of his in very often?'

'Once or twice a week—mostly on a Saturday. Neil and his pals want to hire themselves out as a dance band, so they need quite a bit of practice to be good enough.'

'Couldn't they take turns at practising at their respective homes?'

'That's the snag. Neil's the only one who has his own flat, and the parents of the others can't stand the din, so Neil has them all the time.'

'Oh dear,' said Kitty. 'I'll have to invest in some ear-muffs.'

'The best answer is to have plenty of dates with your boy friends. That's what *I* do. Well, you do have a boy friend?'

'Not a steady one. In fact, there's no

one at present. I'm one of those awkward females, in that I seem to attract only those males I don't particularly fancy. Sad, isn't it?'

'Very,' said Pat, looking at Kitty speculatively. 'We'll have to remedy that. I don't have the men exactly swarming around me, either. My steady, Bob Bingham, is a good sort, but not one to stir the emotions. I guess, with my looks, I can't be too choosy.'

'There's nothing wrong with your looks,' said Kitty, noting Pat's fresh complexion and pleasant expression.

'Ah, but I'm too large. Bob says he likes an armful, but most fellas fall for small, helpless-looking girls, like you.'

'Helpless! I'd have you know I'm anything but. I've been running my father's house ever since Mother died, and holding down a very good job as well, so what's helpless about that?'

'What's your father doing now?'

'He's getting married shortly, and gave

41

my brother and I broad hints that he would like his bride to himself. Understandable, I suppose.'

'So you got the push.'

'You could say that.'

'Well, not to mind. You'll probably have a better time on your own.'

'I think I'm going to miss being part of a family,' said Kitty.

'Before you know it, you'll find yourself married with a family of your own.'

'Perhaps. But I don't want to marry just for the sake of having a family or because I'm lonely. I want my marriage to be something special.'

'Don't we all!' Pat sipped her coffee, then looked at Kitty. 'Let's hope it happens to both of us.'

THREE

The house was quiet and peaceful when Kitty went to bed that night. No band music from downstairs. Not even any traffic noise. Lovely, thought Kitty as she dropped off into a sound sleep.

Some time during the night, she woke to the insistent sound of tapping. It seemed to come from the wall. She lay quietly for a moment, thinking she must have dreamt it. Then there was another tap and a faint voice calling 'Kitty.'

It must be Pat. She remembered now that Pat had mentioned there was only a wall between their two beds. Kitty, now fully awake, put on her robe and slippers and padded out to the corridor. She hesitated outside the adjoining flat and thought she heard a faint moan. She tried the handle and found the door was locked.

'Pat,' she called urgently. 'Are you all right?'

'Just a minute,' Pat answered. The key turned in the lock, the door opened, and there was Pat, bent double and clutching her stomach.

'I feel terrible,' said Pat, her face a grey-green.

'Get right back to bed,' said Kitty, taking her arm. 'How long has this been going on?'

'Hours,' said Pat. 'I think I'm going to die.'

'Could it be something you've eaten?'

'I don't think so.'

'I'll call your doctor. Who is he?'

'I don't have one. I'm never ill.'

'Well, you are now. I'll ring for the ambulance. They have a doctor on board, I believe.'

Kitty picked up the phone and dialled 111. When she'd given the necessary details, she hung up, then found an overnight bag in which she packed, under Pat's feeble instructions, a spare pair of pyjamas and some toilet things. The ambulance was there in five minutes. Kitty had heard it coming down the street, and belted down the stairs to let the men in.

One of them, who had a bag, said to Kitty, 'I'm Dr. Gregory. Where's the patient?'

'Up the stairs.' Kitty ran up, followed by the doctor and two ambulance men, carrying a stretcher.

Pat was lying on the bed, her face contorted with pain and looking very ill indeed.

Dr. Gregory asked her some questions, then prodded her stomach, noting when she winced.

When he straightened up, he said to Pat, 'We'll soon have you better, but we'll have to move fast.' He turned to Kitty. 'She'll need some toilet things. Could you bring them along later?'

45

'I've already packed a bag,' said Kitty.

'Oh, good. In that case, perhaps you could come along with us. Are you her sister?'

'No, just a friend. Her relatives don't live in this city. I'll be glad to come.'

The ambulance men now had Pat on the stretcher and were manoeuvering her through the doorway. Kitty picked up the overnight bag.

'I'll take that,' said Dr. Gregory. 'You grab a coat. We'll send you home in a taxi.'

Kitty rushed back to her flat, snatched her coat off a hanger in the hall and raced down the stairs on Dr. Gregory's heels. He gave her a helping hand into the ambulance, and Kitty subsided on to a narrow seat, unaware as yet that her pyjama legs protruded from her coat which was slung over her shoulders, and that she was wearing only pink mules on her feet. Dr. Gregory was seated beside Pat, keeping a close watch on her.

It was only a few minutes before they reached the hospital, but to Kitty, it seemed ages, because she was quite sure now, that every moment counted as far as Pat's life was concerned.

Pat was admitted to a side room in a ward and was immediately taken over by hospital staff.

After Kitty had given the Sister in charge the necessary details as far as she knew them, she was told that she could go home and could visit Pat the following evening.

Kitty walked back down the corridors feeling as if she were in some sort of dream—or nightmare. When she reached the door of the hospital, a night porter. approached her and told her that a taxi was awaiting her and would take her home.

In the taxi, Kitty became conscious of her pyjama-clad legs and hoped the taxi driver was an understanding sort. He was full of chat and asked her if a relative had been taken ill.

Kitty said, 'No, a friend. I hope it's

nothing too serious.'

'They'll take good care of her at the hospital. I often take in people who look as if they are at their last gasp, and it seems no time before I'm called upon to take them home again, fit and well.'

'I hope that will be the case with my friend,' said Kitty fervently, feeling as if Pat were indeed a friend whom she had known much longer than a day or two.

Back at the flat, Kitty went to bed, but her mind was too active to allow sleep to take over and, at six-thirty she got up, made a cup of tea and sat at the kitchen table drinking it. When she'd finished it, she remembered that Pat's flat was probably unlocked, so she went along and tried the door, which opened.

She tidied up a bit, making the bed and putting away some of Pat's scattered underclothes. On the dressing table she saw Pat's purse.

She hesitated before opening it, but if the latchkey wasn't in the purse, she'd have to hunt for it. There was money, a library ticket and the key all in the purse, and Kitty thankfully snipped the lock and took the purse back to her own flat, guessing that Pat would need it in hospital.

After she'd had breakfast, she straightened her own flat, put Pat's purse in a drawer and, after making sure her own door was locked, went off to work.

At the factory she found the atmosphere one of gloom. The girls in the main office were discussing the dismissal notices. Three of the typists and one of the male clerks had been made redundant, and the talk centred around the prospect of their chances of obtaining other positions.

'How's your job, Kitty?' one of the girls asked. 'I've still got it,' said Kitty, 'but one never knows.'

Her boss, Mr. Chester, also seemed to be in a despondent mood, and hardly spoke to her except to give her some letters to answer.

On the way home at five o'clock, Kitty

bought some flowers to take to Pat when she visited her that evening.

She cooked herself a chop and some vegetables, finishing up with an apple, and then caught a bus to the hospital. She found Pat in a bed just inside the door of the surgical ward. She was propped up against six pillows and when she saw Kitty approaching, she smiled with pleasure.

'How are you?' asked Kitty, putting the flowers on the bedside table.

'All right. It was my appendix. Nice of you to come, Kitty, and thanks for the flowers. They're lovely.'

'I've brought your purse. Is there anything else I can do for you? Anyone you want notified that you're here?'

'I'll write to my parents in a day or two. No use worrying them. They're in Whangarei and they'd think they had to come down to Dunedin to see me, and they can't afford it.'

'What about your boy friend?'

'Bob Bingham? Ring him if you like,

but we're cooling off a bit, I think.' Pat's voice sounded tired, and Kitty caught hold of her hand and squeezed it.

'I'll go now, Pat. I guess you need sleep more than visitors.'

Pat didn't argue the point on that. 'Thanks for coming, Kitty. I appreciate it.'

Kitty walked back along the corridors and, nearing the entrance, almost collided with Dr. Gregory, who put out a hand to steady her.

'Sorry,' he said, beginning to walk away. Then he turned. 'Haven't I seen you before?'

'Yes. In the early hours of this morning. I was in the ambulance with my friend, Pat Matson.'

'Of course. I guess my attention was mainly on the patient. She'll be recovering by now, I guess.'

'Yes, I've just seen her.'

'Good.' He gave her a brief nod and went off.

Kitty's head turned and she watched his retreating back as if mesmerized. His stride and general bearing encouraged confidence and Kitty felt that, if ever she were in an accident, Dr. Gregory would be the one she would like to have on hand. He must be going for a meal in the cafeteria prior to night duty in the ambulance, she surmised.

When she arrived home, Neil Woodward came out of his flat. 'I say, what was all the commotion last night? Did I see the ambulance driving off, or was I dreaming?'

'You weren't dreaming. It was Pat. She had an acute attack of appendicitis and was rushed to hospital for an operation. I've just been to see her. She's all right, but still a bit dopey. I'm hoping she'll be brighter when I see her tomorrow night.'

'I'll come with you. I'll run you there. You haven't a car, have you?'

'No. Thanks, Neil. I'll be glad of a lift. I want to take her a few things—notepaper, stamps and nightwear, I guess.'

As Neil drove her to the hospital that evening, he said, 'I hope we didn't keep you awake with our racket the other night?'

'Well, you did wake me up,' admitted Kitty, 'but I suppose a band has to practise.'

'We're just a pop group, actually. It's difficult to find anywhere suitable to practise. We try not to go on for too long, but sometimes we get carried away and forget the time.'

'Are you aiming to make a living out of it?'

'We're keeping our fingers crossed. We hope to get regular engagements sooner or later, but there's pretty, stiff competition. I say, you don't sing, by any chance?'

Kitty laughed. 'Not really.'

'We need a pretty girl to add some glamour. You'd be just right. Why don't you come down the next time we're practising and try it out?'

'Thanks for the offer,' said Kitty, shaking her head. 'You see, I have absolutely no inclination to perform in public, even if I had the talent.'

At the hospital they went along to Pat's ward and found her sitting up looking reasonably cheerful.

'Am I glad to see you both. I wasn't expecting visitors.'

Kitty put the parcel she had brought on the bed. 'Notepaper, stamps, nightwear,' she explained.

'You're an angel,' said Pat.

Neil produced a bag of oranges. 'Don't know whether you can eat these or not.'

'I'll eat them all right,' said Pat. 'I'm starving.'

'How are you, then?' asked Kitty.

'Perfectly all right. I was hounded out of bed first thing; and here's me thinking one went to hospital to be waited on hand and foot. Not so. And me one of the staff and all. You'd think I'd rate v.i.p. treatment, wouldn't you?'

Kitty beamed. 'It just goes to show you're getting on well.'

'I guess so. The thing is to remember not to make me laugh. It kills me.'

'I heard this joke today ...' began Neil.

'I dare you to tell it,' said Pat. 'Hey, Kitty, did you ring up Bob?'

'Yes. I had to try several times, but I got him just before I came here. He's sorry to hear you're ill.'

'But he's not coming to see me?'

'Oh, I guess he will,' said Kitty, refraining from telling Pat that Bob had said he hated hospitals, but he'd try and remember to send a card.

Pat said philosophically, 'Bob hates any sort of illness, so it'll be a miracle if he turns up.'

At the end of the week Pat was home, having been told to recuperate another week before going back to work. Kitty did the shopping for her and helped with meals and jobs about the house.

One evening, Kitty had a telephone call from her father.

'Kitty, love,' he said, reproach in his

voice, 'I thought you'd have been back to see me by now. I've rung you in the evenings, but you always seem to be out. I hope you're behaving yourself.'

'I'm sorry, Dad. My girl friend next door took ill and I've been at the hospital visiting her. And of course I'm behaving myself. What a question!'

'Well, now I've finally got you, Myra and I would like you and Richard to come to our wedding. It's next Saturday. Three o'clock at St. Luke's church. Very quiet, just a couple of Myra's women friends, and her uncle to give her away. We're having cake and champagne back at the house afterwards. Will you pass on the invitation to Richard? I've tried to get him but haven't succeeded.'

Kitty rang Richard's number two or three times before she contacted him and told him the news.

'Three o'clock Saturday? Can't manage it,' said Richard firmly.

'You'll *have* to.'

'There's no "have to" about it.'

'But I need some support, Richard. There'll be several of Myra's friends, and only me on our side of the family.'

'I'm not coming, and that's that. I have a prior engagement.'

'What's so important that it can't be put off?'

'I'm going out with Marylyn Dollimore. It was sheer hard labour pinning her down to a date and, once having cornered her, one does not cancel that lightly.'

'Well, I'll make your excuses, pathetic as they are.'

'They're not as pathetic as my father getting married again,' said Richard, having the last word, with which Kitty wholeheartedly concurred.

FOUR

Saturday was a bleak day and, although the rain held off, grey clouds, driven by a chill wind, scudded across the sky.

Kitty arrived at the church just before three. It was empty except for the clergyman who greeted her and told her where to sit. The bridal party arrived on time, Herbert and Myra coming in together followed by the uncle and two women friends.

Myra, dressed in rich blue, looked almost regal as she stood at the altar, her head held high. The ceremony began and, when the phrase, 'If anyone knows of any just impediment why this couple should not be joined in lawful matrimony, let him now speak ...' was said, Kitty had to suppress a violent inclination to shout, 'I do.' She couldn't *bear* to think of this woman taking her mother's place and using her mother's things.

She gave herself a mental shake. She must regard the matter sensibly instead of emotionally because Dad, no doubt, would be better off having someone to look after him. If only Myra were likable! She resolved there and then to try and look for Myra's good points.

After the ceremony, they all went back to the house, Kitty being given a lift by one of the women.

Herbert approached Kitty. 'Where's Richard?' he asked.

'He had a very important previous engagement which he said he couldn't possibly break,' said Kitty, straining the truth as she added, 'He asked me to give you his best regards as well as his apologies.'

'What's more important than his father's wedding?' asked Herbert, looking hurt.

'Well, you did give us rather short notice.'

Herbert sighed. 'The young are so full of their own affairs. I suppose it's all I can expect from that young man. How are you managing in your flat, love?'

'Very well, thank you.'

Kitty left the party as soon as she decently could. The place she had regarded as home for most of her life, didn't feel like home any longer. Myra's presence and personality already seemed to permeate the rooms, perhaps because she had substituted some of her own furniture in it.

Whatever had happened to the old familiar pieces, wondered Kitty. Sent to an auction room, no doubt. She could have done with some of them herself.

Back at the flat, Kitty let herself in with her key, divested herself of her best outfit, put on a pair of jeans and a striped red top and then went and knocked on Pat's door.

Bob Bingham opened the door. 'Have

you come to see Pat?' he asked. 'She's on the couch with her feet up. A nice one she is—not letting me know she was in hospital.'

'I'm afraid that was my fault,' apologised Kitty. 'Pat was rushed in so suddenly. I did try to get hold of you, but you were out.'

'I travel for Tennant and Clyde, the leather people, and I had to go away on an unexpected trip.'

'That explains it,' said Kitty, not feeling very impressed with Bob. There was something superficial about him and she felt he wasn't good enough for Pat. Perhaps the fact that he was very tall and well built had attracted Pat to him.

Kitty turned to Pat. 'How are you feeling?'

Pat was making the most of being an interesting invalid. She was wearing a rose-pink negligeé and her hair, instead of being tied back, hung around her shoulders in a soft cloud. She looked like a delicate, Victorian lady who was used to being cherished.

'As you can see, I'm not too bad, Kitty. How come you're home so soon from the wedding? I thought you'd be imbibing champers for some time yet.'

'It was a very short affair,' said Kitty. 'The bride and groom are catching a plane to the North Island at seven, so they wouldn't have appreciated the guests hanging around for too long.'

When Kitty arrived at the office on Monday morning, Mr. Chester rang for her straight away.

'Sit down,' he said when she entered the room.

He looked pale and drawn as if he hadn't slept well.

'I'm afraid,' he went on, 'I have some rather bad news. As you're no doubt aware, the business has been falling away rather drastically. There has been a special meeting of creditors over the weekend, and the company will probably have to go into receivership.'

'I'm sorry to hear that. Does that mean I'm out of a job?'

'We all are.' Mr. Chester ran his hand over his brow. 'Things have been bad for some time and it's been the last straw to lose most of the Australian business. They're cutting down on imports because their own economy is in the doldrums.'

'But what shall we all do?' asked Kitty with a sinking heart. 'Go on the unemployment benefit?'

'There'll be redundancy pay, and I'll give you a good reference. You should have no trouble in finding other employment.'

'But what about you?' Kitty couldn't help asking.

'Well, it won't be easy to get a job at my age. We have a big house and two cars, so we'll probably sell the house and one of the cars and find a more modest type of residence. Well, that's enough of my worries. We'll be busy here, tidying up the ends for about two weeks, but I'd advise you to watch the advertisements and apply for anything you think suitable.'

The following fortnight was a sort of nightmare, the like of which Kitty hoped she would never have to live through again. An atmosphere of despondency emanated from all remaining employees. The redundancy pay wouldn't last forever, and there were too many people applying for too few jobs advertised in the daily papers.

Kitty was glad when it was all over, but felt very strange when, after the final weekend, she had no special reason for getting up on Monday morning. Except, of course, the very good reason of trying to find a job.

Pat, who had read about the company's failure in the newspaper, was full of sympathy for Kitty who assured her there was no cause for pity. She had enough money to keep her going for a month or two. She had prudently put most of her redundancy pay in to the savings bank, keeping out only enough to pay the week's rent and to buy food. She ordered a morning newspaper to be delivered, as this came well before breakfast, and she could read the 'Situations vacant' columns hoping there might be something suitable that she could apply for, and be first in line.

But she soon found out that this ploy had been thought of by dozens of other girls in the same unfortunate position as herself and, after several eager trips to firms offering office jobs, she began to feel panicky at finding herself only one in a hundred.

When she had experienced a week of this, she began to search the paper for more humble jobs. Even a Girl Friday would be better than nothing and, although rather a come-down after a secretarial position, it could lead to better things.

She began economising on food, making a loaf of bread last a day longer than she normally did, and giving herself smaller helpings of meat, which was an expensive item. She bought the cheaper vegetables—swedes and cabbage, knowing they were as full of nourishment than the more expensive peas and beans.

This economy business was something new to Kitty, and she found herself in a situation she had never dreamed could occur. She had lived at home with her parents in security for most of her life and now, here she was, thrust out of that home by a step-mother, and out of a job through no fault of her own. It was enough to make any girl despair.

But Kitty, despite occasional fits of depression, had a resilient nature, and she could not but believe that something good was awaiting her just around the corner.

Richard called in one evening and found Kitty carefully mending a hole in her panty-hose. He threw his long length into a chair and remarked, 'Since when did you start mending those? At home, you always threw them away when they sprang a run.

You're not hard-up, are you?'

Kitty said, 'I've lost my job.'

'You haven't! What have you done? Robbed the cash box?'

'Richard! Surely you saw in the paper that Chester and Wearman have closed down? I've been made redundant—what a horrid word. Sounds like a bit of old junk that's been thrown on the scrapheap.'

'Good lord. I'm sorry about that. I just don't read the papers all the time, I'm afraid. Are you on the dole?'

'No. I'm not reduced to that, yet.'

'There must be plenty of jobs available for an experienced secretary like you. Have you tried applying for any?'

'Well, I haven't exactly been sitting here waiting for something to fall into my lap. I've applied for a dozen or so, but every time, someone else has beaten me to it.'

'Something will turn up,' said Richard cheerfully.

'I wish I could be so sure. I suppose you don't know of anything?'

'Not at the moment. I'll enquire around, though. Why didn't you let me know at once?'

'I didn't want to worry you.'

'Idiot!' Richard rose to his feet. 'Must be going. I say, do you want any help? I haven't much spare cash, but I wouldn't see you stuck. Have you thought of going back home? Dad would let you have your old room for nothing, I'm sure. Paying rent sure eats up the cash.'

'I can't see myself living in the same house as Myra.'

'No, neither can I. Well, it was just a thought.'

Kitty renewed her efforts to find a job. She took to haunting the office of the afternoon newspaper, buying a copy as soon as it came off the press. There were very few secretarial jobs going, so she tried the shop vacancies but, on applying, was told that, as she had no experience behind a counter, she could not be given the job.

Pat, having recovered quite quickly from her operation returned to her physiotherapist job at the hospital, but arrived home every night awfully tired, and fit for nothing but a quick snack and early to bed. She occasionally asked Kitty how she was getting on, but took it for granted that Kitty still had plenty of money in the bank and was not yet in dire straits.

But Kitty became more and more worried. She felt too proud to apply for the unemployment benefit. She paid the rent regularly, but spent less and less on food.

When Myra rang her one Saturday morning and invited her to mid-day dinner, Kitty, who had vowed never to enter the house again, could not resist the thought of a square meal, and accepted with alacrity.

She arrived on time and was assailed at the door by the alluring, delectable smell of roasting meat. At the table, Myra put a plateful of tender roast beef, baked potatoes, peas and beans with a good, rich gravy before her, it was all Kitty could do not to wolf the lot down with animal greed.

'Well, I don't suppose you give yourself good meals like this,' commented Herbert, smiling at his daughter, who was tucking into the meal with every evidence of enjoyment.

'No, I don't,' said Kitty. 'It doesn't seem worth while to cook a roast just for one.'

'Well, we haven't seen your flat yet,' said Herbert. 'And if you invite us to dinner, you will have an excuse to cook a roast.'

'I'll do that one day,' said Kitty, wondering how she could budget her money to provide an expensive meal for three. 'I guess I'm a little out of practice with cooking.'

'I suppose you have most of your meals out,' said Myra. 'That's what I used to do after my mother died. But, still, one never loses the knack of cooking, I always say, and Herbert doesn't complain.'

Kitty went home in the middle of the afternoon without making any firm date for her father and step-mother to visit her. She thought it strange that neither of them had mentioned the closing down of Chester and Wearman, and came to the conclusion that, with so many major businesses going into liquidation, or amalgamating with others, the closing down of Chester and Wearman had escaped their notice.

She should have told them herself, she supposed, but she had refrained, fearing they might think she was hinting that she wanted to return to live with them.

FIVE

There came the day when Kitty, exhausted by trudging around the town applying for jobs, and lack of a decent meal, almost fainted when she went back to her flat at five o'clock one Friday.

She had drawn all her savings from the bank and, when she counted the dollars in her purse, she found there were only twenty left. Not even enough to pay the rent which was due next week. There was nothing left but to apply for the dole. She shrank away from the thought of it. But what else could she do?

She pondered over her problem as she ate her meal of poached egg on toast, and decided to ask Richard's advice. There might even be a vacancy in the newspaper office where he worked as assistant photographer, although she knew he would have mentioned it if it had come to his ears.

She rang Richard's number at seven. Andy Pearce, one of Richard's flat mates, answered.

'Hang on a minute,' he said. 'I'll get him. He's washer-up tonight.'

Kitty heard him call, 'Hey, Rich, there's a dame on the phone for you. Real nice voice.'

There was silence for a moment and then Richard said in dulcet tones, 'Hello?'

'Sorry to disappoint you, Rich. It's your sister.'

'Oh, Kitty.' Richard's voice had returned to it's normal, matter-of-fact one. 'What's cooking?'

'I wish something *was* cooking. Food, I mean. Richard, it's hard to believe, I can't get a job—not even a Girl Friday one. You wouldn't know of anything going, I suppose?'

'No, I'm afraid not. I've been keeping

my eyes open, of course, but things are tough now.'

'I'll have to go on the dole, then.'

'Kitty, you can't! Don't tell me it's as bad as that!'

'It is, you know. I'll have to find somewhere less expensive to live. I can't pay for my present flat on unemployment benefit.'

'Just let me think a moment,' said Richard. 'I suppose you wouldn't consider going back home? No, of course not. I would hate for you to have to do that—not after having been turfed out.'

'I had thought of throwing myself on Dad's mercy, but it would be awful to go back, knowing Myra resented my being there.'

'Listen, Kit. Would you like to move in here? There's a small room off the kitchen that none of us use except for our suitcases. You could earn your keep by taking over the cooking. We find it a bit of a chore—especially the shopping.

I'd have to consult Andy and Des first, though.'

'Oh, Richard. Would you? It would be a lifesaver. I was feeling like a drowning girl going down for the third time.'

'Look, I'll ring off now and talk it over with them. They're both here. Then I'll ring you back.'

'Rich, I do hope they'll agree. One thing, though. No funny business.'

Richard laughed. 'Des and Andy aren't like that. Anyhow, with me around they wouldn't dare.'

They hung up, and fifteen minutes later the phone rang. Kitty, tense with anxiety, picked it up at the first tingle.

'You're on,' said Richard. 'You can move in tomorrow if you like.'

'Saved by the bell,' said Kitty, almost hysterical with relief. 'You're sure they don't mind? You seemed to be ages deciding.'

'Actually, they're pleased. They were just asking me a few pertinent questions about you. We've thought up a scheme. We can't afford to pay you housekeeper's wages, but we'll all muck in and give you a set amount to buy food and stuff, and you can keep what money's left for yourself. But don't give us mince every day just to economise. We would like proper meals. We're a bit tired of living on take aways and such.'

Kitty laughed. 'You won't be sorry. I'll not skimp you in any way. Trust me.'

'It's a deal,' said Richard. 'We'll all come round early tomorrow and shift you in. You haven't a lot of stuff, have you? We'll hire a trailer for Andy's car.'

'I'll be ready and waiting,' promised Kitty. 'What time?'

'About nine. That suit you?'

'Grand,' said Kitty.

The boys arrived at nine, as promised, the next morning. Des Mayes was a school teacher, and Andy Pearce a reporter for the paper Richard worked for.

They looked at her small pile of household goods and suitcases. 'We'll soon make short work of this,' said Andy. 'but what about a bed?'

'Isn't there one?' asked Kitty. 'I mean at your house.'

Richard clapped his hand to his head. 'I quite forgot you'd taken this place completely furnished,' he said. 'Well, after we've unloaded this stuff, Kitty, I'll ring up Dad and tell him we're coming to pick up your bed. Surely you're entitled to the furniture in your own room.'

'You'd better let *me* explain to him,' said Kitty. 'Oh, dear, I hope I'm not being an awful nuisance.'

'Of course not,' said Des. 'While we've got the trailer we may as well make full use of it.'

Kitty rang her father as soon as they reached the big house, and was glad it was he who answered, and not Myra.

Herbert raised no objections, even suggesting that Kitty have the full contents of her old room.

'I know Myra won't mind,' he said.

'She was suggesting that we use your old room for a sunroom. Anyway, I'm glad to hear you're moving in with Richard. I haven't liked the thought of you living on your own.'

When the boys went off with the car and trailer, Kitty had a good look at the room she was to occupy. She had thought that an annex to the kitchen would be a small one, but was agreeably surprised that it was quite large. It had probably been occupied in its early years by a housekeeper.

She happily settled some of her china in the kitchen, glad to see there were plenty of cupboards, and then wandered around the ground floor, revelling in so much space after being confined to a tiny flat. The boys each had a bedroom upstairs, where there was also a large bathroom and wash-basin. Kitty had been told she could have the downstairs bathroom—a much smaller one, with the stipulation that, when the upstairs one was in too great a demand for the three of them, they could, with her permission, use the downstairs one.

After she was settled in, they all sat down with mugs of coffee around the large kitchen table to talk over arrangements. It was decided that each of the boys pay twenty dollars a week to Kitty and, with this, she would provide and cook meals for the four of them, the situation to be reviewed at the end of a month to see if the amount they contributed worked out to everyone's satisfaction.

'Sixty dollars isn't a great amount,' said Des. 'You'll need something for yourself, Kitty, and I guess you were earning more than that at your job.'

'Yes, I was,' said Kitty, 'but at least I have a free home and food, and I do have plenty of clothes, having been rather extravagant in that direction in the past. What I would like to know is if any of you have anything you particularly like or dislike in the way of food.'

'I can't stand tripe,' said Andy, pulling down his mouth.

'And I hate tapioca,' said Des.

'You know my preferences,' said Richard. 'Oh, by the way, we usually come home for lunch and we all enjoy those long, crunchy yards of bread. We cut off hunks and eat them with cheese, tomatoes or what have you.'

'Yes,' said Des. 'We look forward to that every day, so don't go cooking anything fancy for lunches.'

'I'll save all my energies for dinners,' said Kitty, smiling at them. 'What about breakfasts?'

'Cooked ones,' said Richard. 'Sausages, eggs, bacon, toast and coffee.'

'An omelette now and again would go down well,' said Des. 'Are you any good at them, Kitty?'

'Not too bad. Well, thanks, boys. If there's something I cook that you don't fancy, promise you'll tell me.'

'You bet we will,' said Richard.

When they had all gone to work on Monday morning, Kitty bounced around, cleaning and tidying up, thoroughly enjoying having the house to herself. Her spirits were high, because the threat of having to go on the dole had been removed, at least temporarily.

She went to the shops at ten and came home laden with food parcels. It seemed no time before it was twelve o'clock and the boys were home for their mid-day snack which Kitty had ready as instructed—long rolls of crusty bread, cheese and tomatoes, and also a lettuce.

This, she decided, was much better than flatting on one's own. She had free food, no rent, and the company of three lively males.

When a week had gone by, Kitty counted out the money left from the sixty dollars. Just under five dollars. She hadn't spent a penny on herself, and five dollars wouldn't go far when she needed a new sweater or some shoes and undies.

She sat down and made a note of the cost of various items. Breakfast, she found, was almost as expensive as dinner. Eggs and bacon were such a price, and the boys seemed to expect two eggs each. She gave them French toast one morning, and waited anxiously for their reaction to this much cheaper meal. They all approved, so Kitty served it up once a week, sometimes topping it with fried tomatoes.

Pat kept in touch with her and, one Saturday, rang up to ask if she could come and see Kitty that afternoon.

'I wish you would,' said Kitty. 'The boys will be out, I think, so we can have a nice, private chat.'

'That's exactly what I need,' said Pat, sounding gloomy.

'Is anything the matter?' asked Kitty.

'I'll tell you when I see you.'

At lunch time Des and Andy said they were going to the cricket and not to wait tea for them. They'd rustle up something for themselves when they got in.

'Aren't you going, too?' Kitty asked Richard.

'I've got an assignment later on—a wedding—daughter of a member of parliament.'

'That sounds interesting.'

'It's dead boring. Weddings are all the same—smiling bride, nervous groom, proud parents. When *I* get married, no one will know about it.'

'I've got Pat coming. She's a bit under the weather and needs a few comforting words, from what I can gather.'

'Are you hinting that I make myself scarce?'

'Goodness, no. It's your house. We can go to my room.'

'No. I'll go to *my* room. The wedding's at five.'

Pat turned up just after two, and Kitty took her into the living-room.

'It's lovely to see you, Pat. How's everyone at the flats?'

'Neil Woodward's got a new girl friend, and Bob and I have had a flaming row.' She burst into tears.

Kitty was shocked to see sensible, matter-of-fact Pat so upset. 'You'll make it up. You know how things are. Rows happen, and then it's all over, and you're on again.'

'No, it's permanent. Things haven't been quite right between us for some time. Bob was getting restless. I could see that, but I wouldn't accept it.' Then she burst out with it. 'He's found himself another girl.'

'I wouldn't waste any tears on him. You're awfully attractive, Pat. You'll soon find someone else—and probably much nicer than Bob Bingham.'

'Didn't you like him?' said Pat, drying her eyes.

'I didn't actually know him. I only saw him once. To tell you the truth, I didn't form any opinion.'

'The thing is, I don't attract men easily. I'm too big. Men like dainty, little girls—like you.'

'Don't give me that. There is no line of men queueing up to take me out, and never has been. Of course I've had dates, but never anything serious.'

'It doesn't do to get serious. I really thought Bob was the one.' Pat gave a sniffle and then smiled weakly. 'I feel better now, having unloaded my woes on you.'

'I'll make a pot of tea,' said Kitty. 'I actually did some baking this morning to give the boys a treat, so there's chocolate cake, all iced, and a date loaf.'

'How are you coping with them?'

'Fine. I'm still looking for a job, though. The day will come when I need a salary. I don't like to spend the boys' money on myself. Not that there's much left by the time I've bought supplies. Their appetites are not what you'd call delicate.'

Kitty made the tea and then glanced at her watch. 'Goodness, it's half-past three. Richard is dozing in his room. He asked me to call him at four as he has an assignment. He's a photographer, and has a wedding this afternoon. Do you mind if

I bring him in for a cup of tea?'

'Of course not. I did meet him briefly the day you moved out, remember?'

'Oh, yes. I forgot.' Kitty set out the cups, sliced and buttered the loaf and cut the cake, then went to Richard's room, tapped on the door and opened it. Richard was lying on his bed, reading.

'I've made a cup of tea,' said Kitty. 'Come along and have one with us.'

'Right,' said Richard with alacrity.

In the kitchen, where she'd set out the tea, Kitty said, 'You remember Pat, Richard?'

'Yes. How are you, Pat? Got over your operation? Kitty told me about it.'

'Yes. Almost forgotten.'

Richard began to drink his tea, his gaze returning again and again to Pat.

Kitty chattered away, trying to divert Richard's almost fanatical interest in Pat.

Richard said at last, 'You know, Pat, I'd like to do a photographic study of you. You're the perfect Venus de Milo.'

Pat laughed. 'But I've got arms,' she said, extending two shapely specimens.

'Fortunately,' said Richard.

Kitty said, 'Don't forget your assignment, Rich.'

'What assignment?' said Richard, sparing Kitty a brief glance and then returning his gaze to Pat.

'Well, if it's not all that important ...' said Kitty.

'Oh, the blasted wedding! Well, I suppose I'll have to get moving.' He rose to his feet, went to the door and turned. 'Goodbye, girls. Glad to have met you again, Pat.' Then he returned to her, bent over her and looked into her eyes. 'I meant it when I said I wanted to photograph you.'

'I don't know whether or not I want to be photographed,' said Pat, looking pensive. When he'd shut the door behind him, Pat continued, 'Your brother is quite a charmer, isn't he? I bet he's a wow with all the girls.'

'To tell you the truth, I'm utterly amazed. I've never seen Richard act like that before. He's smitten, Pat.'

'Oh, what a pity. And me with a broken heart.'

'Hearts mend.'

'Does he like his job?' asked Pat.

'Yes, he loves it, in spite of his moans about weddings, and the pay is quite good, I believe.'

'I've always thought it would be exciting to be a photographer for a newspaper. One would get involved in all sorts of situations.'

'Yes, there's that side of it, but what he's really keen on is to do photographic studies for competitions. He spends quite a lot of his leisure in seeking out something unusual to photograph. Things like an old stump in a marsh that's thrown a weird shadow.'

'I hope he doesn't regard *me* as an old stump,' said Pat, laughing, adding, 'I say, he wouldn't be wanting to snap me in the nude, would he? If so, it's not on.'

'I shouldn't think so. He's never been one to gloat over the "Miss World" competitions. He says that sort of meat market bores him.'

'Oh, well,' said Pat, 'it will be interesting to see what sort of a pose he thinks up for me, but I wouldn't be surprised if he forgets all about it.'

'He won't,' said Kitty, resolving to nudge Richard's memory if he *did* forget. Pat needed some distraction to take her mind off her troubles.

SIX

Kitty continued industriously to search for work. She had reached the stage when she would do anything, just anything to be earning money. It was humiliating to be dependent on Richard and his friends—as if she were a sponger. She didn't mind how lowly the job was—scrubbing floors, being a postie or an attendant in a ladies' room; anything, as long as it was honest work.

Richard began to see quite a lot of Pat, and frequently brought her to the house for a meal. Kitty couldn't have been more pleased and hoped the relationship would continue to develop, as she could think of no one nicer than Pat for a sister-in-law.

After dinner one evening, Pat was

chatting about something that had happened at the hospital as she and Kitty did the dishes.

'You enjoy your work, don't you, Pat?' said Kitty.

'I love it. One meets all sorts.'

'I only wish I had taken up something like that. It's such a safe position. The hospital will never go out of business.'

'Ah, but if I were to make too many mistakes, I'd be out on my neck.'

'I suppose you had to go through quite of lot of training?'

'Yes, but I don't think my sort of work would suit you, Kitty. It's fairly strenuous, actually, and you're so small.'

'I suppose there's nothing else I could do there, say in the office?'

'I could inquire, but all the jobs are advertised in the papers. The only vacancy I know of at the moment is in the doctor's cafeteria, and you wouldn't want that, I guess.'

'Oh, yes I would,' said Kitty. 'Pat,

you've saved my life—that is, if they'll take me.'

'You wouldn't do a job like that, would you?'

'Oh, yes I would. It's easy to see you've never been out of work. You can't imagine how desperate one feels—unwanted, redundant, useless. Anyway, a cafeteria job would be no different to what I'm doing right now, cooking and washing up for the lads.'

'Well,' said Pat dubiously, 'the cook's a hard one to please. She's always sacking the girls.'

'Then I'll just have to prove that I can do better than any she's had in the past, won't I?'

Pat rang Kitty up the next morning and said she had made an appointment for her to see Mrs. Hoddy, the cook. It was for three o'clock that afternoon.

'Be there on the dot,' warned Pat. 'And make your hair go as flat as possible, and wear your plainest frock.'

'Right. And I'll scrub my face with soap and water to make it all shiny—no make-up. How's that?'

'Terrific,' said Pat. 'Now, don't forget. Be prompt, and good luck.'

Kitty spent a feverish morning sorting through her clothes and finally decided to wear a plain, dark blue frock with a neat, striped collar. She tried her hair in different styles. It was naturally very wavy but, after slicking it down with some of Richard's hair cream, she subdued the waves sufficiently to make her hair lie almost flat.

She arrived at the hospital well before three and had just entered the lobby and was looking about for the enquiry desk when an ambulance arrived. There was an air of urgency as the ambulance attendants came in, carrying a stretcher beside which walked Dr. Gregory.

His eye caught the figure of Kitty standing wide-eyed, and he turned his head briefly as if puzzled as to her identity, and then became immediately absorbed in his patient.

He didn't remember her, thought Kitty, even though they'd been together with Pat in the ambulance. And she'd seen him when she'd visited Pat. But, of course, doctors saw so many people—relatives of patients and such, they couldn't possibly take an interest in all of them.

Nevertheless, she did feel a twinge of hurt that she could so easily be forgotten, especially by one whom she, herself found attractive.

Then she remembered her slicked down hair and shiny, pink face. No wonder he'd looked puzzled for a moment before he'd switched his attention to his patient.

At the enquiry desk she was told where to go to be interviewed by Mrs. Hoddy, and she went along the corridors and finally located the doctors' cafeteria. Mrs. Hoddy had a small office off the large, shining kitchen with its big cooker and long, benches.

Kitty knocked timidly at the office door and waited until a voice called, 'Come.'

She went in. Mrs. Hoddy, who was making out a list, continued to write. It gave Kitty a chance to study her. She was a roly-poly woman with iron-grey hair pulled back and wound into a neat bun. She wore a starched, white uniform and her round, red-veined face was creased with tiny lines.

'These dieticians think they know better than me,' she muttered as she wrote another item on her list. Then she looked up and regarded Kitty, her gaze shrewdly assessing her applicant. 'I gather you're after this job in the cafeteria? Have you any experience?'

'Not in a cafeteria,' said Kitty. 'I have had plenty of experience in my own home. I looked after my father and brother for a couple of years after my mother died.'

'Oh, well, it doesn't take much experience to pour out tea, and make sandwiches. The thing is, are you used to standing on your feet? You don't look particularly robust to me.'

'But I am,' said Kitty. 'I'm never ill. I did have an office job, but my firm went out of business.'

'And I suppose you regard this sort of position as a come-down, eh?'

'I'll do my best to be satisfactory. I consider that any job one undertakes is worth doing well. In fact, I'm looking forward to it. That is, if you take me on,' she finished lamely.

'If you think you'll be chatting up the doctors, you're mistaken. They're very busy people, and all they want from the cafeteria staff is quick service. They're in and out of the caff in nothing flat.'

'I quite understand,' said Kitty. 'I'll aim at becoming as dead-pan as the tea urn.'

Mrs. Hoddy tut-tutted. 'No need for that. A cheerful face is a great asset, so reply pleasantly if you're spoken to. But know your place. You can start as soon as you like.'

'Tomorrow?'

Mrs. Hoddy looked up at Kitty's beaming face and her mouth twitched up at the corners. 'Eight o'clock sharp, half an hour for lunch, and you finish at three-thirty. I hope your enthusiasm stays with you.'

'Oh, it will. Thank you, Mrs. Hoddy.' Kitty turned to go, then hesitated. 'What do I wear?' she asked.

'Uniforms are provided.'

Kitty walked out on air, a smile still lighting up her face. She had a job. Hooray! Hooray! She didn't even need to borrow money from Richard to pay for her uniform. She didn't have to go on the dole. Who, in their right mind wants State assistance? It was *everything* to be responsible for oneself. She was her own woman again. Life was wonderful.

It was only fifteen minutes walk from the hospital to home, so she wouldn't have to depend on buses, which would be a saving. Passing a butcher's shop, she went in and brought four, large, expensive steaks on the strength of soon being able to contribute to the household expenses.

Richard, Andy and Des arrived home almost simultaneously, each in turn sniffing the air appreciatively.

'Something smells good,' said Richard. 'Do I detect the rousing odour of steak and onions?'

'The very *best* steak,' said Kitty. 'I felt like lashing out because, guess what, boys? I've landed a job. Now I won't have to be a burden on anybody.'

'Well, I never,' said Andy. 'Tell all.'

'Later,' said Kitty. 'I'm dishing up right now. Get yourselves washed and brushed, pronto.'

As they ate the meal, Richard said, 'Well, out with it, Kitty. Where's this fabulous job?'

'At the hospital,' said Kitty.

'Doing what? You haven't trained as a nurse.'

'In the cafeteria, making sandwiches and

serving tea and coffee to the doctors.'

'You can't do that,' said Richard.

'Who says I can't? It's honest work.'

'Maybe so, but you're trained for better things. Why waste your talent?'

'Don't be stuffy, Richard,' said Kitty, not wanting to be damped down. 'What have I been doing right here for the last few weeks but to wait on you three?'

'She's right,' said Des.

'What hours are you working?' asked Richard.

'Eight to three-thirty, and weekends off.'

'But who'll get our breakfasts and cook the dinners?'

'You looked after yourselves quite well before I came along. We can each get our own breakfasts and you can help me with the dinners, that is, if you still want me here.'

Des said, 'Of course we want you here. Richard is just being difficult because you've spoilt us all with your good meals. He's thinking mainly of his stomach.'

Andy said, 'Well, I think this calls for congratulations. Well done, Kitty. I like to see someone with enough spunk to take on a job they're not used to, just to be independent. And, you never know,' he added with a grin, 'you might get off with one of the doctors.'

'According to my boss, Mrs. Hoddy, I'm to be part of the furniture—no getting chummy with the high-and-mighty doctors,' said Kitty.

The next morning was a bit of a scramble for Kitty, as she had to leave the house at twenty to eight. She'd set the table the night before, but left the boys to get their own breakfasts as arranged.

At the hospital, Kitty presented herself to Mrs. Hoddy who said, 'Well, I'm glad you're on time. I just hope you keep it up.' She went to a linen cupboard and brought out a white overall. 'Put this on, it's a small size and should fit, then Doreen will show you what to do.' Mrs. Hoddy glanced at the clock on the wall. 'She's late, as usual.

It's gone eight, but she should be here at any minute.'

At that moment, the door opened and a thin dark girl with bright brown eyes and a sallow complexion, came bursting in. 'I'm not late, am I, Mrs. Hoddy? I snagged my panty-hose and had to change them at the last moment. If only we were allowed to wear slacks, a snag wouldn't matter.'

'That's not the attitude to take, my girl,' said Mrs. Hoddy. 'A girl who is careless about her underwear is careless about other things. Now, listen, Doreen, I've a helper for you.' She indicated Kitty. 'This is Kitty Willet—Doreen O'Reilly.'

'Hello,' said Doreen, smiling and showing slightly crooked, white teeth. 'Am I glad to see you! Yesterday was hectic. I had to manage on my own. It's a wonder I made it at all today, I'm so tired in the legs, being on the go as I was.'

'Now, stop complaining, Doreen,' said Mrs. Hoddy. 'Get your overall on and then show Kitty what to do.'

Doreen was soon into her overall. She indicated a large table by the wall. 'We work here, starting on the sandwiches. Mrs. Hoddy likes to keep the big table to herself.'

'I should think so,' said Mrs. Hoddy, overhearing. 'With all I've got to do, I must have plenty of space. I can't abide being cramped.'

Doreen fetched several loaves of brown and white sliced bread, butter, a roll of ham, a slab of corned beef, hard boiled eggs, lettuces, and tomatoes, and then fetched several large trays.

'We make the sandwiches,' instructed Doreen, 'and we put them on these trays, then cover then with damp muslin and, just before ten, we put them in the glass cases on the caff counter.'

The time flew past, and by nine enough sandwiches had been made for morning tea. Mrs. Hoddy had been busy making a variety of scones—cheese, date and plain, and these were cooling on wire racks, waiting to be buttered.

'We'll start putting out the sandwiches now,' said Doreen, 'and we keep the damp cheesecloth on until it's time for the first arrivals.'

The cafeteria was furnished with about a dozen formica-topped tables, four chairs at each.

'Is this big enough for all the doctors?' asked Kitty.

'Well, they don't all come in together,' said Doreen.

'I guess it would be chaos in the hospital if they did,' said Kitty. 'What about lunches? Is it just sandwiches and scones?'

'Goodness, no. It's as good as a hot dinner, but we do put more sandwiches out for those who want just a quick snack. There'll be more kitchen staff arriving to do the vegetables and to help with the dishing up and, after that, with the washing up. We won't be involved in that unless someone's off ill. We do have to clear the dishes away and keep the tables clean. Now, come and have a look at the Zip water heaters. You have to be sure they don't run empty, and when you fill them you keep your eye on the indicator so they don't overflow. When they boil, they scream like mad.'

By a quarter to ten, the first few doctors began to arrive. Kitty soon got into the swing of things, filling cups with either tea or coffee. They all seemed to be in a hurry and sat at the small tables with their colleagues only as long as it took to swallow a sandwich and a drink.

It was getting on for eleven o'clock and the cafeteria was almost empty when Kitty saw Dr. Gregory approaching. She wondered if he would recognise her with her slicked down hair and shiny skin when he saw her at close quarters.

'Tea, please,' he said as he filled a plate with two sandwiches and two scones. 'Didn't have time for breakfast.'

As he accepted the tea from Kitty, he

looked at her closely. 'I know you, don't I? Didn't you come in the ambulance with your girl friend a week or two back?'

'Yes,' said Kitty.

'What are you doing here?' he asked in obvious surprise.

'I work here,' said Kitty.

'Oh,' he said. 'Then I'll be seeing more of you, I expect.' He walked with his tray to a far table by the window.

Doreen said, 'Do you *know* Dr. Gregory?'

'Not really. I came to the hospital in the ambulance with my girl friend when she was taken ill with appendicitis. Dr. Gregory was the accompanying doctor.'

'Fancy him remembering you! He should have had all his attention on your friend, poor suffering thing.'

'Well, he did. He spared me only a passing glance, but some people have good memories for faces, and he must be one of them.'

'I bet he wouldn't remember *me* if he

met me in the street.'

'Of course he would. He's got those see-all, remember-all eyes. Let's hope he hasn't got hear-all ears.'

'He's too busy reading that journal. Swotting, I suppose.'

'What do we do now?'

'I'll clear the tables while you stack the empty sandwich trays.'

Doreen was still busy wiping down tables when Dr. Gregory returned to the counter and handed over his tray.

He said, his brow creased into a frown, 'You're not used to this type of work, are you?'

'Do I appear to be incompetent?' countered Kitty mildly.

'Let's say you look highly intelligent, and cafeteria work doesn't exactly stretch the brain.'

'I suppose you could say I'm a victim of the economy. My firm had to close down. I was secretary to the manager and I was made redundant, as the saying is now.'

'Pity. There's too much of that happening right now, Miss ... er ...'

'Katrina Willet.'

'I'm Ian Gregory. Well, I hope you'll soon find a job suitable to your abilities, Miss Willet.' A brief smile flashed across his face as he nodded and strode away.

SEVEN

When Kitty arrived home that afternoon, she went to her room and changed her dress, then brushed her hair and fluffed it back into its waves, then regarded her face critically. So Dr. Gregory thought she looked highly intelligent, did he? It was a compliment, but she grudgingly admitted to herself that she would prefer to have been called pretty.

She was frying chops, onions and tomatoes when Richard came in.

'How did the job go?' asked Richard.

'I like it. Quite a change, of course, from office work, but it's so lovely to be *employed* after chasing jobs for weeks. You don't know the feeling ...'

'I can imagine,' said Richard. 'I say, Kit, I rang your pal, Pat Matson, and asked her round tonight. I asked her if I could take a few shots of her, and she's agreeable.'

'It'll be too dark in the garden, won't it?'

'I asked her to come early. It won't be dark until after eight. I'm going to take a few inside shots with flashlights, as well.'

'Not nude ones, I hope.'

'Of course not. I'd be too embarrassed to try anything like that, even if she was agreeable.'

'I'm sure she wouldn't be—not that I've known her for long, but I do like her very much. By the way, she's had a row with her boy friend, Bob Bingham, so perhaps posing for you will give her a fresh interest in life.'

'I'm not much good at mending broken hearts,' said Richard, 'so don't expect me to console her. I merely see her as a subject for my camera. Hey, perhaps it was that quarrel that gave her such a pensive, wistful look. I'd better take advantage of it before her heart mends.'

'You're callous!' said Kitty indignantly. 'All you care about is getting a good picture and never mind Pat's upset love-life.'

Richard grinned. 'It's the artist in me, love. Anyway, I like Pat. She's got something in her—a depth of character. She'll be good to look at when she's old and grey.'

Pat arrived just as the sun was setting. Richard urged her into the back garden to take a picture of her against a birch tree which was showing tender green leaves. Pat was wearing a filmy, white frock and Kitty thought she looked delightful.

The faint shadows under her eyes, caused by the faithless Bob, gave her a look of touching vulnerability, and Richard, who did not care to take pictures of toothy, smiling people, took every advantage of this. There would be no telling her to say 'cheese', or 'look pleasant, please.'

Kitty, glancing out of the kitchen window, did hope the photographs would be successful, because, Richard, she knew, was hoping to enter some pictures in a competition that was coming up.

After the photographic session, Pat stayed and chatted for a bit. The cheerful banter of the boys made her forget her own troubles, and Kitty was glad to see the old sparkle back in her eyes.

After a cup of tea and biscuits, Pat rose to go, and Des said, 'I'll run you home.'

'No need,' said Richard hastily. 'My car's at the gate.' He glanced at Des with a steely eye.

'I thought you'd be wanting to develop your film,' said Des.

'I'll do them at the office in my lunch hour. Better equipment,' said Richard.

When they'd gone, Des said to Kitty, 'Do you think old Richard is smitten?'

'I don't know. He's never had much time for girls, but I suppose it could happen, and who better than Pat?'

'She's a good looker. Tall, but fragile.'

'She's not usually like that. When I first

met her, she was big and bouncy, but her appendix operation slimmed her down. I imagine she'll be back to normal before too long.'

'Has she a steady boy friend?'

'She did have, but that's over now.'

'Ah! A pity it takes an illness and an unhappy love affair to give a girl an air of mystery and fragility.'

'Well, I'd prefer to see her happy and blooming, even if it does put on a few pounds.'

Kitty and Des were still talking companionably when Richard returned an hour later.

'Well, my boy,' said Des. 'It took you a long time to say goodnight.'

'We got talking,' said Richard. 'Any objections?'

'Why should I have? Kitty and I were doing the same.' He got up and stretched his arms above his head. 'Time we were all in bed. Andy hit the sack long ago.'

He went off while Kitty pottered about,

straightening cushions and folding the evening paper neatly.

Richard sat astride a chair watching her absentmindedly. Then he said, 'I think I'm in love, Kit.'

'With Pat? Oh, Richie, how wonderful! But you said taking the photos of her was only a job of work and you had no interest in her otherwise.'

Richard, his arms folded on the back of his chair, tilted it to an alarming degree. 'I feel I really got to know her tonight. A chap can change his mind, surely.'

'Were there any signs that she reciprocates? I do hope she does. I'd love to have her for a sister-in-law.'

Richard sighed. 'It's rather too soon to hope for that. She's hardly recovered from her blighted hopes about that swine, Bob Bingham.'

'M-mmm. I suppose it would be better not to rush her. But, honestly, Rich, a bit of attention from a nice chap like you should give a much needed boost to her ego. And one thing leads to another, and before she knows it, she'll be thinking less and less about Bob, and more and more about you.'

'I suppose this Bob was a much better looking fellow than me?'

Kitty regarded her brother, trying to view him without prejudice. She never thought about his looks. He was just Richard. Yet, with his big, strong frame, unruly dark hair and firm jaw line, she supposed he would have considerable attraction for the opposite sex.

'Well, I guess Bob did have a surface charm,' she said. 'But I saw very little of him, so I'm no judge. Anyway, Rich, if you pursue this course of taking photos of Pat, you will have a legitimate excuse to take her out without her thinking you are being too pressing. You're always looking for unusual backgrounds, so go ahead, take her out and about.'

'I say, I think that might work. I'll keep it all on a casual, friendly basis.

But wouldn't she think it a cheek for me to expect her to give up her time to pose for me?'

'Good heavens, no. She'll be flattered. Anyway, Pat would soon say if she found it a bore. She's not devious like some females I know. Myra, for instance.'

Richard said, 'Have you heard anything from Dad lately?'

'Not since I went there for dinner. Oh, my goodness!' Kitty clapped her hand to her forehead. 'I was supposed to reciprocate and invite them for a meal, but I've been so caught up in my own affairs, I quite forgot. Should we have them here, do you think?'

'I'd like to say no, but I suppose there's no sense in keeping up a feud. Dad's married to that woman, and she *is* our step-mother. Ask them if you like.'

'Perhaps we could arrange it for one night when Des and Andy are out.'

'I think I'd prefer to have the boys here, too, then Dad couldn't reproach me for failing to turn up at their wedding.'

'And all because of a date with some dolly-bird. What was her name? I gather you haven't seen her since.'

'Marylyn Dollimore.' Richard gave a laugh. 'She was just a flash in the pan. But what a flash!'

Kitty rang her father the next day. 'I'm living at Richard's house now, Dad. I'm sorry I didn't tell you sooner, but I've been very busy looking for another job.'

'We wondered what had happened to you. Well, thank goodness you've rung. I only heard the other day that your firm had closed down. Have you managed to find something else?'

'Yes. I'm working at the hospital.'

'Not nursing? You've had no training for that.'

'No. I'm helping in the cafeteria.'

'That's a bit of a waste for one of your qualifications, isn't it?'

'It's better than being unemployed. I had a taste of that for a week or two and I didn't like it one bit. Dad, the reason I'm ringing is to ask if you and Myra would care to come and have dinner with Rich and I and his flat-mates.'

'Just a minute. I'll ask Myra.'

Kitty could hear their voices in the background, murmuring together, and finally her father returned to the phone. 'Yes, we'd love to come. What day?'

'Tomorrow at six?'

'Yes, that will be fine.'

'See you then.' Kitty told him the address.

'Right. We'll find it. Er ... Kitty, I've missed you, love.'

'You too, Dad.'

Kitty hung up, feeling remorseful that she hadn't kept in touch with her father more often. She had been acting like a spoiled infant to grudge him a little happiness in his later years.

The dinner party the next evening was not a roaring success. There seemed to be no common interest between Herbert and Myra and the boys. They talked spasmodically of the weather, the inflation of the economy and the Government, on which there were decidedly opposing views.

Kitty dredged up a few comic incidents which had occurred at the hospital, but it was a relief for all when the meal was over.

Des and Andy insisted on doing the dishes and afterwards, made their excuses and went out.

Sitting over a second cup of coffee, Myra remarked that it was a big house for Kitty to keep clean.

'But we all share the chores,' said Kitty.

'I'm glad to hear that,' said Myra. 'I'm not at all in favour of mixed flatting. It wasn't even thought of in my young days.'

'But Richard's here, which puts a different light on it,' put in Herbert. 'I can't say I approve of couples shacking up together, but I suppose we're behind the times, dear.'

'And behind the times we shall stay. Morals mean nothing nowadays,' said Myra primly.

Kitty and Richard heaved a united sigh of relief when Herbert and Myra went home.

'What Dad sees in her I fail to comprehend,' said Richard.

'The stiff, starchy side she shows to the world might be different to the one she shows Dad. She might be all softly feminine when they're alone.'

'It's hard to imagine.'

'Well, we've got that visit off our chests,' said Kitty. 'I'm going to bed.'

EIGHT

The boys had arranged an all-day tramp for Saturday, but Kitty, on being asked to join them, said she would rather stay at home as she had various small jobs she wanted to catch up on.

She helped pack their lunches and, when they had gone and she was tidying up the living-room, she was struck by its rather drab appearance. The wall-paper wasn't bad, plain cream, and the carpet, though thin and flattened, was a soft green. Her gaze riveted on the linen slip-covers of the fat-armed sofa and chairs. They were dull and grey-looking. She studied them more closely and discovered there was a pattern of flowers of some sort. What they needed was a trip to the cleaners. Then it occurred to her, why not do the cleaning herself?

No sooner thought of than done. She had the covers off in no time, unzipping them from the back. Underneath was a covering of genoa velvet, worn bare in places.

Kitty filled one of the old-fashioned concrete tubs in the laundry with hot water, adding a generous amount of soap powder and whipping it up into frothy suds. She dunked in the covers and left them to soak, while she vacuumed the house. Then she returned to the laundry and tackled the covers, rubbing and scrubbing at them with a bar of soap.

It took three changes of suds and water to release the dirt from the covers, but when she had struggled outside with them and hung them on the clothes-line to flap in the breeze, she was delighted at the way the colours had come up in the linen.

They took hours to dry and almost as long to iron their awkward shapes into smoothness. But finally she had them back on the sofa and chairs. They certainly gave the room a lift with their design of soft pink roses and mauve sweet peas against a cream background, and they gave off a sweet-smelling scent of cleanliness and fresh air.

Richard, Andy and Des returned hungry from their tramp and, after a good meal in the kitchen, they all went into the living-room. Kitty followed, wondering if they'd notice any difference. It might not be apparent to them.

But she was not disappointed.

Des said, 'What's this? Have you been buying new furniture? Hey, they're nice, but where did you get the money?'

Richard and Andy were equally open-mouthed.

'Have you been to an auction sale, or something?' asked Richard.

Kitty, a broad smile across her face, said, 'They're the same covers, actually. They've just had the dirt of ages washed out of them.'

'I wouldn't have believed it,' said Andy.

'You'll make someone a good wife,' said Des. 'If it wasn't for my Sally, I'd be inclined to chase after you.'

Encouraged by this success, Kitty cast a speculative glance around the kitchen. It was designed to accommodate the large families that were in vogue when the house was built. Before embarking on any decoration, she consulted with the boys, who agreed that it could do with some new paint, but that the owner of the house would have to be consulted first. They also suggested that they make it a communal effort and get the job done quickly.

The owner, Mrs. Parker, was an elderly lady who had moved out of the house into a flat some years ago. She offered to pay for the paint, admitting that it would cost her a packet if she had to pay a tradesman.

Within a week, the drab fawn and dull green paintwork in the kitchen was superseded by much lighter colours, mostly lime green and white. The boys clubbed together and bought a couple of multi-striped rugs for the floor, and Kitty contributed some white pottery jars in which she planted small ferns for the adornment of the wide window-sill.

The result of this exercise was that each of them felt they now had a place they could be proud to bring their friends.

When Kitty arrived at the hospital one morning, there was a commotion in the admittance lobby. An ambulance was being discharged of accident victims, and Dr. Gregory was assisting in their despatch to the appropriate units.

Later, he came into the cafeteria and approached the counter where Kitty was busy setting out cups and saucers for morning tea.

'Good morning,' he said, 'I'm rather early, but could I have a cup of black coffee, as strong as you can make it?'

'Yes, certainly,' said Kitty. 'It won't take a moment. The zip's on the boil.'

When she handed him the steaming cup, she noted that his shoulders, usually so erect, sagged dispiritedly.

'Have you had a busy morning?'

'Have I ever! It takes a strong stomach to look on some of the sights I've encountered. It's not so bad when one can patch them up and set them on the road to recovery, but when it's a small child, like today ...' His voice trailed off.

'Is he going to get better?'

'No. It's over for him. And not his fault. He wasn't the careless one. When parents allow their child to stand on the front seat of the car, and then have to brake suddenly ... God, what fools some people are. Sometimes I wish I'd never taken on this job. I would like to be a member of Parliament and make strict rules about careless drivers. The hospitals wouldn't require half the staff if it weren't for the carnage on the roads.'

Dr. Gregory stayed at the counter to drink the coffee. He seemed to feel a need to talk, and Kitty's eyes expressed concern and sympathy.

'Can I get you a sandwich?' she asked. 'They're all ready.'

'No, thanks. The coffee is what I need.' He stood there silently while Kitty continued to set out the cups.

When he set down the empty cup, he said to Kitty with an appeal in his eyes, 'Would you come out with me tonight? I'm afraid I'm not very good company at the moment, but I'd like to get right away from the hospital atmosphere.'

Kitty said impulsively, 'Would you come to my place for dinner? I live with my brother and his two friends. We all take turns with the cooking, and it's my turn tonight.'

The expression on Dr. Gregory's face lightened. 'I'd love to do that if it won't cause you any trouble.'

'Of course it won't. I'm not a gourmet cook, but I can promise you a good, tender steak.'

'Just the thing the doctor ordered.' He delved in his pocket and brought out a notebook. 'Now, what's your address, or can I give you a lift?'

'I finish at three-thirty, so I'll be home before you're ready.' She told him the address, and Dr. Gregory went off.

No sooner had he gone than Kitty began to panic. What on earth had possessed her to ask one of the doctors to dinner? And all because he looked pathetic and upset.

Kitty worked hard all day and at twenty-five past three she approached Cook. 'I've finished, Mrs. Hoddy. May I go now?'

Mrs. Hoddy glanced at her watch. 'If the whole staff in this hospital took five minutes off every day, it would add up to quite a few hours, you know.'

'Yes, but I did arrive five minutes early this morning,' countered Kitty.

'Oh, well, just this once, then.'

Kitty hurried off, stopping at a block of shops to collect meat, vegetables and, from a home bakery, a large apple tart.

Dr. Gregory arrived soon after five.

'Not too early, am I?' he asked Kitty when she opened the door.

'You're first, but the others won't be long.' She took him into the living-room. 'I've still got things to do in the kitchen, so if you'll excuse me ... There are some magazines on that table.'

'Can I come into the kitchen and help? It's ages since I've done any chores like that.'

'I'd welcome some help,' said Kitty. 'There are some peas to pod and they take ages.'

In the kitchen she indicated a seat at the large table and put a brown paper bag and a saucepan in front of him.

'I couldn't resist buying these fresh ones. They have a different flavour to the tinned or frozen varieties.'

'I fervently agree.' Dr. Gregory began to pod the peas, putting one in his mouth now and again. 'I say, my name's Ian. Would you please call me that?'

'Well, while you're here, I will, but not at the hospital.'

He grinned. 'Very discreet, I see. You're Kitty, aren't you? I've heard that other girl, Doreen, isn't it, call you that.'

'Yes, short for Katrina.' Kitty laid several pieces of steak on a wooden board and beat them with the end of a rolling-pin.

'Why are you hammering them to death?' Ian's voice was mildly curious.

'To break down the fibres and make them tender.'

'Well, of course. I should have known.'

The vegetables were simmering and the steaks sizzling when Richard came in the back door.

'Do I smell steak?' he asked hopefully.

'You do. Richard, we have a guest for dinner. This is Dr. Ian Gregory. He does ambulance duty.'

Ian rose to his feet and he and Richard shook hands.

'We must have come close to meeting, at times,' said Richard. 'I often have to take accident photos for my paper, but often, by the time I get there, the ambulance has gone and there are just these wrecks of cars.'

'I sometimes wish,' said Ian with heartfelt sincerity, 'that photos of some of the accident victims would be printed. It might horrify people into being more careful when they're driving. It's that "one-for-the-road" drink that often makes a good driver into a bad one. However, I suppose it's better not to print pictures of the victims. It would be too harrowing for the relatives.'

Andy and Des came in, were introduced to Ian and, when they had washed and brushed their hair, they all sat down at the table, doing full justice to the meal that Kitty had cooked.

Afterwards, the boys switched on 'Softly, Softly', a T.V. programme they followed avidly. Kitty was amused when, after fifteen minutes of this, she noticed that Ian's head had dropped on to his chest and he was fast asleep.

She indicated this to the boys with a finger to her lips, and they let him sleep on, turning down the T.V. volume so they could just hear it, and refraining from making any conversation.

It was almost ten o'clock when Ian stirred, opened his eyes and looked around in a dazed way at his companions.

'I must have dropped off for a minute,' he said, looking at his watch. 'Is that the time? I say, that was amazingly bad manners on my part. I do apologise.'

They all laughed, and after a moment, Ian joined in.

When the laughter had subsided, Ian said, 'Why on earth didn't you wake me up?'

'You looked so peaceful, and you must have needed the rest,' said Kitty.

'As long as you don't infer it was our boring company that put you out,' said Richard.

'You may take it as a compliment,' said Ian. 'It was partly due to the fact that

I worked late last night owing to my colleague not being available, but mostly because I feel so at home here.' He grinned at them in an apologetic, endearing way.

'I'll make some coffee so you won't fall asleep driving your car home,' said Kitty. She rose and went to the kitchen.

Ian followed her. 'Let me help,' he offered. 'I feel wonderful now. So relaxed and happy somehow.' He looked around him. 'This is a lovely, homey kitchen.'

'We've just done it up,' said Kitty, setting out coffee mugs. 'Where do your parents live?'

'In Australia. I have a sister there whose husband was killed in a car accident a few months ago, and she really needed them, so they uprooted from here, and went. I think that was the reason I wanted to do a stint on ambulance work. If only a doctor had been on the scene earlier, he might not have died.'

'What an awful thing,' said Kitty. 'It was bad enough when my mother died, but she did have every care.'

'How does your father cope? Is he in this town?'

'Yes, he married again recently. That's why Richard and I moved out. The second wife wanted Dad to herself—natural, I suppose.'

'But hard on you.'

'I did feel a bit put out at the time, but I must admit I'm enjoying flatting—if you can call it that. The boys were used to taking turns with the chores before I joined them and, having got the habit, they still go on doing it, whereas, some males, like my father, think that cooking and housework are solely woman's work. I *have* taken over the shopping, though, but simply because I have shorter hours and more time to visit the shops while they're open.'

'Do you work out the menus, too?'

'We usually discuss that together. Luckily, all three boys enjoy cooking, especially at the weekends, and we have some weird and wonderful dishes.'

'You all seem to get on well together.' There was a note of envy in Ian's voice.

'Yes, we do. Each of us is free to come and go as we please and if friends are invited for a party, we all pitch in. But they haven't had any parties lately. Des is swotting—he's a teacher—and Richard is usually developing photos in the shed. He's made part of it into a dark room. He does some of them—anything special—in his lunch hour at work because the equipment is better.'

After they'd had the coffee, Ian said he must go, and Kitty accompanied him to the door.

'Look after yourself, Ian,' she said lightly.

'Do you care what happens to me?'

'Of course I do—the same as I do about all my friends.'

He looked down at her. 'I was hoping it would be especially me, but thank you, anyway.' He put both his hands around her face and kissed her gently on the mouth, then went to his car and, with a wave of his hand, drove off.

When she went back to the living-room, Des said, 'We like your boy friend.'

'He's not my boy friend. He's a doctor, and I'm just a skivvy in the cafeteria.'

'He wasn't too exalted to accept an invitation for dinner from you,' said Richard. 'Ah, well, he has now learned, having met us, that you're kin to superior beings.' He thumped his chest in lordly fashion.

'How we do like ourselves!' Kitty rumpled her brother's hair affectionately.

The next day at lunch-time, Dr. Gregory came into the cafeteria earlier than usual and approached Kitty who was setting out cups at the counter.

'I must apologise for my dreadful behaviour last night,' he said, *sotto voce*, with a glance at Doreen who was engaged in putting platters of sandwiches in the glass case.

'There's not a thing to apologise for,' said Kitty, wondering whether he meant his lapse into sleep or his farewell kiss. She hoped it wasn't the latter.

'I can assure you I won't let such a thing happen again. Do you forgive me?'

'It's a perfectly natural phenomenon—sleep—especially when one is over-tired.'

'Thanks for taking it like that. About that dinner I was going to take you to. Are you free on Wednesday night?'

'I'd love to come,' said Kitty, hoping she did not sound too eager. She was beginning to like Dr. Ian Gregory more and more.

NINE

Later that afternoon, when they were wiping down tables, Doreen said to Kitty, 'Did I hear you being invited out to dinner by Dr. Gregory?'

'You must have sharp ears, Doreen. Yes, he did invite me out to dinner, but don't read anything into it.'

'I'm glad you said that. We girls have to keep these young doctors in their places. They like a bit of fun, but that's as far as it goes.'

'I'm aware of that,' said Kitty. 'How about you? Have you a boy friend?'

'No. I'm in between, so to speak. The last one I went out with wasn't up to much, so I told him to get lost. I don't like going out with no-hopers because you're only keeping other boys off. Actually, I *have* met one or two I think I could go for, but the trouble is, *they* don't fancy *me*. Isn't it difficult being a girl?'

'It certainly is,' agreed Kitty. 'Well, not to worry. I guess we'll both get married sooner or later, and then we'll wonder why we ever got up such a head of steam worrying about Mr. Right turning up.'

'Oh, *you'll* have no trouble,' said Doreen. 'You've got the right sort of looks.'

'If there are queues of eligible men lining up to propose marriage, I've failed to notice them,' said Kitty. 'Anyway, I'd like to stay single a while yet, and I'd advise you to do the same, young Doreen. You don't know when you're well off.'

Mrs. Hoddy came out from the kitchen. 'What are you two girls nattering about? It's high time you were finished.'

'Nearly done, Mrs. Hoddy,' said Doreen cheerfully. 'Kitty and I were discussing our marriage prospects. Did you have much trouble hooking Mr. Hoddy?'

'Percy Hoddy had to do a lot of

persuading to get me to marry him, I can tell you that. And he was a lucky man, even if I say so myself, with me earning a good living and being a good cook and all.'

It wasn't often that Mrs. Hoddy opened up about her own life, and Kitty said tentatively, 'Yes, he was lucky, Mrs. Hoddy. What does he do for a living?'

'He works for the council—keeps the streets tidy and such. He and his mates fill up any pot-holes and do asphalt work where needed. But they don't kill themselves, believe me. Half the time they're leaning on their shovels swapping yarns, from what I hear. And all at the expense of the ratepayers. But that's men for you. Wouldn't ever do a hand's turn if they could get out of it. By heck, if they got through as much work in a day as I do, the rates would drop by half.' She went back to the kitchen, muttering to herself.

'Such sweeping statements!' said Kitty, giggling. 'What is her opinion of our poor, overworked doctors? Or aren't they men?'

'Not in her book,' said Doreen. 'To her they're super-human.'

Kitty tried, at various times, to find another secretarial position, but with no success. For every job advertised, as many as a hundred girls applied.

She was not too unhappy about this, as she was enjoying life at the cafeteria and, even if the work didn't stretch the brain, there was plenty going on to make things interesting, far more so than in her previous place of employment.

When Wednesday came around, Kitty felt more and more elated at the prospect of dining with Dr. Ian Gregory. She made an appointment at the hairdressers for four o'clock.

It was Richard's turn to cook dinner, and his usual menu was fish and chips which he expected his flat mates to eat out of the paper they were wrapped in, saying they tasted much better that way, and didn't have a chance to get cold. No one minded this because it eliminated the chore of washing dishes.

The tantalizing smell of the fish and chips aroused Kitty's appetite, and she helped herself to a fat chip from each of their packets.

She decided to take plenty of time to make herself attractive for her date and, leaving the boys to finish their meal and do the dishes, she had a shower then, back in her room chose her nicest frock—a midnight blue one with billowing filmy sleeves caught in at her slender wrists by narrow cuffs.

Not bad, she thought as she looked critically in the mirror. Quite glamorous in fact and a pleasant change from the plain-Jane image she presented in the cafeteria. Would Ian approve? She went into the living-room to wait for him.

'My, you are dolled up,' remarked Andy. 'I hope he appreciates you.'

'I hope so, too,' said Kitty, 'but I'm under no illusions. This date is just a return compliment for the dinner he had here.'

'Big things sometimes start in small ways,' said Andy.

'You have a romantic nature, Andy.'

'Of course I have—and not ashamed of it.'

'Why don't you find yourself a nice girl and settle down?'

'I can't afford to—yet, but one day I will. How about you waiting for me, Kit?'

'I'm not your type, and you know it,' Kitty smiled at him with affection.

Richard had gone out to his dark room to develop some film, and Kitty and Andy had the living-room to themselves.

As eight o'clock came and went, and then half-past, Kitty began to get restive.

'I think I'm being stood up,' she remarked.

'Well, come out with me, then. I'll dress up and take you to dinner.'

'You've had dinner.'

'Only fish and chips. I could always toy with a lamb chop while you went through the whole menu. I could pretend I was slimming.'

'If you slimmed, you'd be marked absent. You haven't an ounce of spare fat on you.'

'Well, what about it?'

'No, thanks, Andy. It's kind of you to offer, but Ian might turn up after we've left. Doctors do have emergencies cropping up, especially in Ian's particular line.'

'If that had been the case, he'd have rung you up, surely. Or if he was *too* occupied, he could tell some underling to ring you.'

'Yes,' said Kitty doubtfully. 'Yes, he really should have sent me a message if he's unduly delayed. He becomes so involved in his work, I guess he just forgot.'

Kitty picked up the evening paper and settled herself to read it. There was nothing of particular interest, and at nine o'clock she cast it aside.

'I'm starving,' she said. 'I'm going to have something to eat. All I had for lunch was a bowl of soup and a bread roll. No afternoon tea. Starvation doesn't agree with me.'

'There aren't any left-overs,' said Andy. 'The cupboard's practically bare, except for our breakfast.'

Kitty opened the fridge door and peered inside. She came out with a couple of eggs and some cheese. She enveloped herself in an outsize apron that hung on the kitchen door and was in communal use. Ten minutes later she was sitting down to a large, tasty omelette.

'You should have done one for me, too,' said Andy.

Kitty, cross and near tears, said, 'You've *had* your tea. What's left in the fridge is for breakfast.'

At ten o'clock, she went to her room, undressed and climbed into bed, trying to console herself with a library book. As if a mere book, even an exciting one, could compensate for a cancelled or forgotten date and a dull evening at home, she thought bitterly.

When she turned out the light, she lay awake for a long time, listening for the phone and hoping, even at this late hour, for an explanation from Ian. Then she overslept and was woken up by Richard, who urged her to bestir herself if she didn't want to be late for work.

Arriving at the cafeteria, she found Mrs. Hoddy in a bad mood. Doreen had rung up to say she had a cold and wouldn't be in.

'You'll have to work twice as hard,' said Mrs. Hoddy. 'Rona can give you a hand when the rush starts—not that I can spare her, but I'll manage somehow.'

Rona Smithers, the kitchen-hand, was a gangling, sixteen-year-old with her dark brown hair permed into the tight curls that were currently in fashion. It stood out round her head making her pale face look thinner than was normal.

Kitty buttered bread and filled sandwiches at top speed, placing them on the trays and covering them with damp muslin. When she stationed herself at the counter just before ten o'clock, Dr. Ian Gregory was the first to appear. He approached the counter and regarded Kitty worriedly.

'Sorry about last night,' he said. 'You guessed what happened, of course.'

'I'm afraid I didn't,' said Kitty coldly. 'A phone call might have helped as I'm not clairvoyant.'

'You *must* have heard about the accident,' said Ian incredulously.

'What accident?'

'Don't you listen to the radio?' Ian hurriedly picked up a plate and helped himself to a couple of sandwiches while Kitty poured his coffee. 'Now listen ...' A queue had begun to form and there were mutters from his colleagues urging him to move along as they hadn't all day.

'See you later,' murmured Ian, and went off with his tray.

Kitty glanced at his retreating back. He didn't look as if he'd had an accident. He was as sound in wind and limb as she was. She served the waiting customers while her mind went round and round. Then it dawned on her that it wasn't Ian who'd had the accident, but he'd had to attend one. How dumb could she be? Nevertheless, he surely could either have rung her or commissioned someone else to do so.

He would have to come up with a very good explanation, and she hoped it would be soon. She kept her eye on Ian as she went on with her work, hoping for a word with him when the queue at the counter had thinned. Surely he would come over when he had finished his morning snack.

But before he'd emptied his cup, the intercom boomed out—'Calling Dr. Gregory, Calling Dr. Gregory. Report to Casualty, Dr. Gregory.'

She saw him leap up from his chair and hasten out of the cafeteria. What a life, she thought. Not even a cup of coffee in peace. No wonder some doctors didn't live to ripe old age.

She was wiping down the tables some time later when a young, probationer nurse came in.

She approached Kitty and said, 'Are you Miss Willet?'

Kitty straightened her back. 'Yes.'

'I was to give you this.' The girl proffered an envelope and then went off.

Kitty looked at her name sprawled across the envelope, then put it in her apron pocket. She didn't want Rona Smithers' curious eyes on her when she opened it.

When she'd finished tidying up the tables she went to the bathroom area, shut herself in one of the lavatories and then opened the envelope. Her eyes quickly scanned the hurried scrawl.

'Dear, dear Kitty. Can you please forgive me for not turning up last night, owing to an unexpected set of circumstances? Will explain later. Ian.'

It would have to be an extraordinary set of circumstances for him to be unable even to ring, thought Kitty, somewhat, but not altogether, mollified. What could possibly have occurred? He was supposed to have gone off duty at five. Other doctors would surely take over, even in the event of a bad accident.

She could not help hoping that Ian would manage to come in and see her before she left the hospital. Lunch-time was a rather inconvenient time for explanations. But Ian didn't even appear for lunch. He must be inundated with accidents. Perhaps he would call at home tonight.

She had the dinner cooking when Richard came in. He poked his head round the kitchen door. 'One extra for dinner,' he said. 'Will it stretch, Kit?'

'Who is it?' Surely Ian hadn't arrived for dinner.

'It's Pat.'

'Well, bring her in. Of course the dinner will stretch. It's stew. I'll reinforce it with a packet of mixed vegetables.'

Richard came into the kitchen with his arm through Pat's.

'Are you sure I'm not making things awkward?' Pat asked Kitty.

'No, silly, I'm thrilled to see you. Have you quite recovered from your operation?'

'I've forgotten all about it,' said Pat. 'How are you getting along in the caff? Not finding it too menial, I hope.' Pat seated herself on a kitchen stool.

'To tell you the truth,' said Kitty, 'I enjoy it better than working in a dull, old office. There are more interesting things going on.'

'Such as Dr. Gregory? Is he still pursuing you?'

'Not so's you'd notice,' said Kitty.

'M-mm. It's as well not to take any of the young doctors seriously,' said Pat, echoing Doreen's advice.

After dinner that night, Andy, who

was helping Kitty stack the dishes, said casually, 'How about you and me going to a show tonight? There's a group on in the Town Hall.'

'Thanks, I'd love to,' said Kitty.

Andy looked at her, amazed. 'Are you actually saying "yes?" '

Kitty laughed and then said primly, 'Do you wish to withdraw your offer?'

'No, of course not. I'm delighted, if somewhat startled. Has that doctor friend of yours done the dirty on you?'

'Dr. Gregory leads his own life and I lead mine. A friendly meal at our house doesn't mean a thing. Andy, I'm not making a convenience of you, if that's what you're thinking.'

She sounded convincing, even to herself, and Andy said, 'Well, let's enjoy ourselves, eh?'

'Oh, wait a minute. We've got a guest. I can't walk out on Pat.'

'We'll ask them to come, too.' He turned as Pat came in with more dishes. 'How about you and Rich coming to a show at the Town Hall tonight?'

Richard, who had followed Pat in, said, 'Would you like to?'

'I'd rather not. I still need to go to bed early, although I'm quite fit. You don't mind, Richard?'

'I'd prefer to stay here,' said Richard. 'You two go off and enjoy yourselves.'

TEN

At the theatre, Andy and Kitty managed to get two fairly good seats. There were several pop bands performing and Kitty was astonished to read in the programme that Neil Woodward's group was giving one of the items.

Kitty pointed this out to Andy. 'That must be the Neil Woodward who had a flat right under mine at my last place of abode. His group used to practise a lot, and nearly drove me to distraction.'

'They're not too bad,' said Andy, when Neil's band performed.

'Yes. They've improved quite a lot since I last heard them.'

The whole concert seemed much too noisy to Kitty, as amplifiers increased the volume. The only advantage was that it effectively smothered any nefarious thoughts she would be having about Dr. Gregory, which would have happened if she'd stayed quietly at home.

The next morning, Kitty woke up with a migraine—most unusual for her, and she put the cause down to the terrific din she'd been subjected to the evening before. The thought of having to stand on her feet at the cafeteria for most of the day was too much, and she got Richard to phone Mrs. Hoddy that she would not be in, trusting that Doreen would be back.

Richard, having convinced Mrs. Hoddy that Kitty was much too indisposed for work, took a couple of aspirins and a cup of tea to Kitty, who was still in bed.

'How did Mrs. Hoddy take it?' she asked when she'd swallowed the aspirins.

'She sounded slightly put out, but she said she'd try to get someone to take your place.'

'I hope she doesn't sack me,' said Kitty,

memories of her jobless days still haunting her.

'She won't do that. No one can help being sick, and you do look a bit peaky, old girl.'

'It's these zig-zags before my eyes. Typical of migraine, I've heard, so it's nothing to worry about, but I wouldn't be much good at pouring tea and coffee. I'll be all right in an hour or two, I guess.'

'Are you sure you'll be all right by yourself?'

'Yes, I'll probably sleep it off. The place will be nice and quiet.'

After the boys had gone, Kitty actually did fall into a deep sleep and woke to find it was after one o'clock. Her headache had disappeared as if by magic. Perhaps she should go to work. But the worst of the rush would be over and, by the time she showered, dressed and got to the hospital, it would be almost time to come home.

She made herself a sandwich and a cup

of tea and, feeling the need of some fresh air, went into the back garden.

There were some thundery clouds about and the sky looked as if it could unload some rain before very long. Kitty found a gardening fork and began to work in an overgrown patch of the vegetable garden. In half an hour she had forked over a sizeable patch of rich, dark soil, and began to plan enthusiastically for the sowing of various kinds of vegetables. It wasn't too late in the season for lettuces and tomatoes. What a pleasure it would be to be able to pick one's own.

There was an old shed by the back fence, and she rummaged around in that and found a rusty tin containing some seed packets. They were dated 1975, which would probably make their germination a risky business. Nevertheless, she planted radish, lettuce and spinach seeds and decided to buy some tomato plants at the weekend. The exhilaration of doing something creative had cleared her headache completely away, and she felt on top of the world.

When the boys came home, they found a good dinner of steak and kidney pudding and apple crumble waiting for them.

'What about this headache?' said Richard. 'I thought you were a cot case.'

'I do feel rather a fraud,' said Kitty, 'but this morning I was really under the weather.'

'I woke up with a slight headache myself,' said Andy. 'Those bands were a trifle overpowering. Next time, Kitty, I'll take you to something a little more classy.'

Kitty, who had had her ears strained to the phone, hoping for a call from Ian, was frustrated when Richard rang Pat, and kept the phone engaged for over an hour.

The doorbell rang at eight o'clock and Andy, who answered it, came back with Dr. Gregory following him.

'A visitor for you, Kitty,' Andy said.

'Oh, hello,' said Kitty.

'I'm sorry to drop in unheralded, but I

did try to phone you.'

'The thing is,' said Kitty, 'we each need a phone. I'm afraid my brother is rather long-winded when he's talking to his favourite girl friend.'

'I didn't see you at lunch time,' said Ian. 'Are you all right?'

'Andy took me to a pop show last night,' said Kitty. 'I guess the clanging symbols were a bit too much for my eardrums. I woke up with a nasty headache.' Kitty looked at him obliquely, rather pleased that he now knew she hadn't moped at home, waiting for him to turn up.

'How's the head now?'

'Completely recovered. I've even done a stint in the garden, which refreshed me somewhat.'

'Well, how about some more fresh air? A run in the country?'

Kitty couldn't resist. 'I'd love it. Just wait and I'll fetch my jacket.'

'Better make it a raincoat. There are some ominous clouds behind the hills.'

'M-mm. Perhaps we're in for a thunder-storm. Hasn't your car a hood?'

'It's a convertible, but I thought, as it's warm, it would be fun to have the top down.'

Soon they were riding along in the low-slung car, Kitty wearing a green light-woollen skirt and matching polo-necked top. Her red rain-coat, complete with hood, lay across her knees.

As they headed out of town, Ian said, 'I've a lot of explaining to do.'

'I guessed what had happened. That accident kept you busy, I suppose. But were you too busy to get someone to ring me?'

'Ah! I *am* in deep water. Yes, it was the accident, but one can't very well ring when the accident happened rather far from a phone. Anyway, I was much too involved with the injured bus passengers to think of anything else.'

'You were *at* the accident? I thought ...'

'Yes, I went with the ambulance. It saves

161

time and lives if the injured can be treated before they're moved to hospital. It's the usual procedure to send a doctor along with the ambulance nowadays.'

'Of *course*. Now I understand. I'd quite forgotten that.'

'It was too late by the time I got back and finished patching up the patients at the hospital. I was working until the small hours.'

'I must admit I did think some rather hard thoughts about you for standing me up, which was idiotic of me, as I might have known something unsurmountable had cropped up to detain you.'

Ian grinned down at her and patted her hand. 'It's a hard life, being a doctor. His private life is always having to be relegated to the background. Why did I choose such a profession?'

'You know you wouldn't be happy doing anything else.'

'I guess not, but it's tough on one's girl friends, as they're bound to be inconvenienced at times.'

How many girl friends did Ian have, wondered Kitty with a pang of jealousy. A nice-looking man like Dr. Gregory, she imagined, would have plenty waiting to step in if one girl ditched him.

They were climbing one of the hills surrounding the harbour, leaving the populated area behind them, and Ian pulled in to the verge and halted the car.

'You can see the city lights from here,' he said.

'Let's get out,' said Kitty, suiting action to the words.

There was a stillness in the air that was uncanny. Not a sound anywhere—so different from the continuous hum of city streets. They stood looking at the lights and the reflections in the harbour for a while, then Kitty said, 'Let's walk round that next corner.'

When they reached it, they felt a stirring of a breeze from the south-west. It quickened quite suddenly, and the black cloud that had been stationary began to travel. Then, with a warning clap of thunder, it seemed to open and pour a great burst of water on them.

'Quick!' Ian seized Kitty's arm and hustled her to the car. 'Put on your raincoat while I wind up the hood,' he directed.

Kitty soon had her mac on, but Ian, struggling with a recalcitrant hood, was having difficulties.

'Shall I give you a hand?' Kitty, without waiting for an answer, ran round to the other side and began to tug in earnest. Slowly, the hood yielded to their united efforts and came up.

Inside the car, Ian breathed a sigh of relief, 'Thank goodness for a little shelter, but it's a draughty old bus. I'll be getting a new one when I'm in general practice. The ambulance is my main mode of conveyance in my present job, but meanwhile, this old crate gets me hither and yon.'

He pressed the starter. There was a whirr, but the engine didn't catch. Ian tried again. The same whirr, but feebler.

'Oh, don't tell me the old girl is going temperamental on me.'

'Is she subject to these fits?'

'Occasionally, but she usually picks a place not too far from a garage.'

'Perhaps you're out of petrol,' suggested Kitty.

Ian looked at the gauge. 'I filled her up yesterday. Don't tell me she's sprung a leak. No, there's plenty of petrol, and in any case I always carry a tin of gas in the boot. Perhaps I'd better look under the bonnet.'

'You'll get soaked.'

'I'm pretty wet already. I've a torch somewhere.' He felt in the glove box. 'Ah, here it is.'

'I'll get out and hold it for you.'

'No. I'll prop it up if I have to use both hands. No sense in two of us standing in the rain.'

Ian got out of the car and soon had the bonnet up. In the light of the torch, Kitty saw his features drawn into concentration lines as he peered at the car's innards. He examined everything thoroughly, tightened a screw or two, then put down the bonnet and got in the car.

'Keep your fingers crossed,' he said as he turned on the engine and pressed the accelerator.

The car made the same defeated whoomph as before, then relapsed into silence.

Ian tried a dozen times, but the motor was completely dead. 'I guess the battery's flat, and there's nothing I can do about that. Great heavens, what a fool you'll think I am. Everything I try to arrange for us turns into a disaster. What must you think I am!'

'Human, thank goodness.' Kitty belted her raincoat more tightly around her waist, pulled the red hood well down over her brow and got out of the car.

'There's nothing for it, but to walk,'

she said logically. 'We can hitch a ride, surely.'

'I can't imagine there will be much traffic on this road. It's purely scenic from here on.'

'Oh, come *on*. If we go back the way we came, we'll be in the populated area in no time. Let's look on it as an adventure.'

Ian had one last try at the motor. 'No, go,' he said. 'Very well, we'll try walking. You're a very good sport, Kitty, darling. I can imagine what some girls would have called me if I'd put them in this situation. By the way, how are your shoes—high heeled?'

'No, they're not too bad. Lucky we hadn't planned to go dancing, or I'd have been forced to walk home barefoot.'

'If we'd been dancing, we'd have also been near a phone and could have called a taxi, dope.' He put his hand firmly under Kitty's arm. 'Forward march!'

They plodded along the road, the rain pelting down in their faces, and Kitty would have slipped down in the mud if it hadn't been for Ian's strong arm holding her upright. The wind was at their backs and they made fairly good progress. But as for their hopes of seeing a car, it was that time of evening when not many people were about, and the thunderstorm would deter many from joy-riding.

'We'll stop at the first lighted house we see,' said Ian, 'and ask if we can ring for a taxi.'

After half an hour's walk they reached the first of the houses. It was in darkness, but the second one had a hall light on.

'We'll try this one,' said Ian. 'It has a telephone wire, so they can't refuse, surely.'

They climbed half a dozen steps to the front door and Ian rang the bell. They heard it chiming inside. No one appeared, so Ian rang again.

'They're probably looking at television,' said Ian, pushing the bell again.

This time they heard footsteps approaching and the rattle of a chain being put on the door which then opened a bare two inches. The worried face of an elderly lady squinted at the sodden pair.

She said, 'Go away or I'll call the police,' then slammed shut the door.

'I wouldn't have believed it,' said Kitty as they trudged back to the road.

'I gather we must look rather odd, and she probably lives alone,' surmised Ian.

'She didn't even give us a chance to say what we wanted.'

'Perhaps the next place will be more helpful,' said Ian.

But Kitty had spotted a phone box. 'Look,' she said, her footsteps quickening, 'Let's call a cab.'

Inside the lighted booth, they were squashed together like herrings in a tin. It was a merciful relief to be out of the teeming rain even in such restricted quarters.

Ian struggled to get his hand in his

pocket and finally managed to bring out the necessary coins while Kitty searched the book for the number of a taxi service.

'I could call Richard,' she suggested.

'No. It's not fair to bring him out on a night like this,' said Ian.

'He may be out, anyway. I think they were all going out.'

Ian got through to the taxi service and ordered a cab, only to be told they were all out, there being an excessive demand owing to the downpour but they promised to contact one on the radio telephone, as there was probably one in the vicinity.

He related all this to Kitty and they decided to wait in the booth out of the wet until they saw the taxi.

Kitty pushed back her hood, dug a handkerchief out of her pocket and attempted to dry her face on the small square of linen.

'I think I can produce something more adequate than that,' said Ian and, after a lot of squirming, he brought out a folded handkerchief from an inner pocket. He shook it out and then dabbed at her face.

'I bet I look a sight,' mourned Kitty.

'You sure do. Like a drowned kitten. Hey, that's apt.'

They both laughed, and then jumped as an angry fist hammered on the glass panel of the booth.

The door was pushed open a crack and a man demanded, 'Come out of there. That's no place for canoodling. I need to use that phone urgently. My Tessie's having pups and she's in trouble. I want to ring the vet, but my phone has gone dead.'

'Perhaps I could help,' said Ian. 'I'm not a vet, but I've trained as a doctor and I think you will agree the procedure is not much different in dogs and humans.'

'Come on, then.'

'Where do you live?'

'Just around the next bend.'

Ian and Kitty followed him, and they were taken into the basement of a house built on a steep slope.

'There she is,' said the man, indicating a brown spaniel that was lying on a blanket, whimpering pathetically.

'I'll need to wash,' said Ian.

'There's a wash-basin right behind you, and a towel on the hook. It's quite clean,' said the man.

Ian took off his wet coat, thoroughly washed his hands and then turned his attention to the spaniel. Kitty couldn't bear to look while Ian put all his skill into delivering the pups, but the owner had no such qualms. He squatted down opposite Ian, giving his opinion as to how the job should be done and at the same time, patting the dog's head.

After ten minutes, Ian sat back on his heels. 'That's the lot. Five nice pups,' he said. He went to the basin and washed his hands again, then turned to the man. 'We'll be off, now,' adding diffidently,

'Could you possibly run us to a taxi stand?'

'I'm sorry,' said the man, 'but my car's out of action. The garage can't get the necessary parts for another week.'

'We'll be on our way, then. Goodbye.'

They began to walk off, and the man spared them hardly a glance, waving a vague hand at them in farewell. His attention was entirely with Tessie and her pups.

'He might at least have offered us a cup of tea,' growled Kitty, when they were once more walking down the road.

'Some people just don't think. I should have got his name, then I could have sent him a whopping bill for maternity services rendered.'

They heard a car coming along the road. Ian turned around and, clutching Kitty's arm, waved for it to stop, but, after a slowing down, the driver went on at an increasing speed.

'We must look like disreputable tramps,'

commented Kitty.

'It could have been a lone woman driver, and it is exceedingly unwise to pick up strangers.'

'But surely she could see I was a woman.'

'You look more like a young lad at the moment. There's no way of telling what you are.' Ian squeezed her arm. 'I'm glad you're not a young lad, though.'

Another phone booth loomed in sight. Kitty made for it.

'We haven't the right change, remember?' said Ian.

'We can try pressing button B,' said Kitty, pushing the door open and pressing the button.

Miraculously, the coins clattered out. Kitty triumphantly inserted them and rang Richard. She let it ring for some time, then a sleepy voice answered.

After some argument, Kitty hung up and turned to Ian. 'Richard, the lion-hearted is on his way. He's not too happy about it as he'd just got in and was taking a shower.'

'Well, thank goodness our troubles are over—I hope,' said Ian.

ELEVEN

Kitty and Ian stayed in the shelter of the phone booth until Richard's old car came chugging up the hill.

'What's all this?' he asked, as he surveyed his sister and her escort with disapproving eyes.

They both started to explain at once, and Richard broke in crossly, 'Oh, leave it until we get home. No one but a blithering idiot would be out on a night like this.'

'We'll both sit in the back,' decided Kitty, 'then we won't be squelching up your girl friend's seat.'

'Suit yourselves,' said Richard.

'I'm awfully sorry, Richard,' said Ian, 'but there is a perfectly good explanation.' This overture was met with a stony silence.

Kitty felt a wave of embarrassment at

Richard's curt manner, but the weather was atrocious and hazardous for driving, so Richard's mood was understandable.

As they neared the inner suburbs, Ian said, 'Could you drop me somewhere near the hospital, Richard?'

'Right you are.' Richard was beginning to recover from his ill-temper.

Ian felt for Kitty's hand and squeezed it. 'You're to have a good hot bath when you arrive home and then go straight to bed, and perhaps Richard will bring you a hot drink.'

'Richard needs a hot drink himself,' stated Richard from the front seat. He drew up at the hospital gates.

Ian, as he got out, said, 'Thanks awfully for your help, Richard. I'll do the same for you one day, if the necessity arises.'

'Thanks, but I'll see to it that it doesn't arise.'

When brother and sister were proceeding on their way, Kitty said, 'I know it's annoying to have to do the good Samaritan act on a night like this, but did you need to be so ungracious?'

'I suppose it was the usual ploy of running out of petrol.'

'It was not. We got to the top of the hill and stopped to admire the view, and we could see the storm coming up, so we put up the hood and got in, and the dratted thing wouldn't start. There was plenty of petrol—even a spare tin in the boot. Ian tried everything he knew ...'

'Which wasn't much, I assume.'

'Anyhow, he's going to arrange for a breakdown truck to pick it up tomorrow.'

'Oh well,' said Richard, seeing reason at last, 'I guess it was just one of those things that can't be helped. But why doesn't he get a new car?'

'He intends to when he can afford it. They cost money, you know.'

'I thought doctoring was a lucrative business.'

'Well, Ian had to put himself through med. school and there's such a lot to be spent on equipment et cetera.'

'Doesn't the hospital provide that?'

'I guess so, but he'll need his own instruments when he sets up in practice for himself.'

'Did he tell you all this?'

'Some—but the rest I got from the grape vine.'

'It's a very healthy plant, I gather.'

'You could say it's inclined to rank growth.' Kitty giggled. 'The yarns you hear! They become exaggerated out of all proportion.'

Richard turned the car in their own gateway.

'Here we are. Now hop off inside and run that hot bath just as your doctor friend advised you,' said Richard. 'I'll bring you something good and hot to drink when you're in bed.'

Later, as Kitty sat up in bed, sipping the steaming mug of cocoa Richard had brewed, her hair washed and rubbed dry and a primrose woollen bed jacket over her shoulders, she thought back over the evening, expecting to find her feelings about Ian somewhat cooled in view of their disastrous outing. After all, it was his fault for not having his car checked regularly. Instead, she found herself warming to him. The authoritative, doctor image she knew and respected in hospital surroundings, was now overlaid by a completely human and vulnerable being such as herself.

Kitty suffered no ill effects from her soaking, but when back at work was perturbed that Dr. Ian Gregory failed to appear in the cafeteria. When he was still absent the next day, Kitty made discreet inquiries of one of the other young doctors, Bruce Atkins.

'Oh, he's got a real stinker of a cold. He's confined to his room and has been ordered not to mix with anyone, especially patients, in case he passes it on.'

'I'm sorry about that,' said Kitty innocently, 'I didn't know there was any 'flu about.'

'It's not 'flu exactly. His car broke down while he was out with some dame, and they both got drenched walking home, so I believe. Don't waste your sympathy on him,' he added, grinning. 'He's a tough rooster and he'll recover.' He gave her a second look. 'Hey, it wasn't *you* he was out with?'

'Yes, it was.'

'So you're lacking an escort. How about me? I'll take you out on the town tonight if you like.'

'I don't like,' said Kitty shortly. She passed him his cup of tea and turned to the next customer.

In spite of Bruce Atkins' light dismissal of Ian's cold, Kitty couldn't help but feel anxious about him.

When she had finished work for the day, she went to the residential block and asked at the desk for Dr. Gregory.

'You can go up and see him if you like,' said the woman in the office. 'I don't know whether I should allow you or not, but now you're here, you may as well. He's sure to be feeling sorry for himself. He's number twenty on the first floor. A visit from a pretty girl might hasten his recovery.'

Kitty climbed the stairs and walked along the corridor until she found number twenty. She tapped on the door. There was no answer, and she tapped again.

This time a muffled voice said, 'Enter.'

She went in and saw the prone form of Ian lying on the bed. On seeing her, he sat up with alacrity.

'Kitty! I thought it might be one of the chaps, but am I glad it's you! How did you manage to get past the dragon downstairs?'

'She didn't seem to have any objections,' said Kitty, approaching the bed. 'She inferred I might be a tonic. How are you, anyway?'

'Just a streaming cold. Don't come too near unless, of course, you've got a cold, too.'

Kitty smiled. No, I haven't. I'm sorry

about yours, Ian. You must be feeling miserable.'

'No, not now. The sight of your lovely face has charmed my blues away.'

'Is there anything I can get you?' asked Kitty.

Ian indicated a jug of lemon drink on his bedside table. 'I'm supposed to take plenty of fluids, but I'm rather tired of lemon and barley water. There's a small kitchen just two doors along. Could you make me a cup of tea?'

'I'll do that. Won't be long.' Kitty soon found the small kitchen with its tea-making equipment and in ten minutes was back in Ian's room with two steaming cups of tea.

'I've helped myself to one, too. I hope it's allowed.' She placed Ian's cup on his bedside table.

'That's what the kitchen is for.'

'Yes, for you doctors, but not, I presume, for visitors.'

'Now, don't quibble. Sit over there

well away from me. I'm full of germs.' Ian unfolded a clean, white handkerchief, gave a resounding blow on his nose and wiped his streaming eyes. Then he picked up his cup, sipped the tea and sighed with bliss.

'This is just what I fancied. You know how to make a good brew, Kitty. Are you quite sure you've had no ill effects from your soaking? I feel very guilty about letting you in for such a drenching.'

'I followed your advice and took a scalding hot bath followed by a hot drink, administered by Richard, and that must have done the trick. By the way, how about your car?'

'I rang a break-down service before I was smitten with this cold, and they were picking it up first thing this morning and arranging for repairs—that is, on condition it's worth repairing. I only hope I'm not faced with having to buy another car.'

'Be like me and take to a bike.'

'I didn't know you rode a bike.'

'Only if I'm running late. I like the walk if I've the time.'

'How about a bicycle built for two? The trouble is that bikes don't like steep hills, and there are plenty of those in this city.'

'Luckily, the route to our house is fairly flat, so there's no problem.' Kitty rose to her feet. 'I guess I'd better be going. I hope you're soon better, Ian.'

Ian grinned at her. 'Thanks awfully for coming to see me. It's made my day.'

Richard came bursting into the house soon after five that evening. He found Kitty in the kitchen organizing a meal.

'Guess what!' he said.

Kitty spared him a brief glance. 'By the look on your face, you've won the art union. Or maybe the big lottery?'

'Better than that. Try again.'

'You're going to be knighted.'

'I've declined that honour with thanks.'

'Let's not play guessing games. Just tell me.'

'Right. Pat's agreed to marry me!'

Kitty abandoned the custard she was stirring and turned and stared at him. 'No! Oh, Richie, that's great news. I couldn't think of anyone nicer for a sister-in-law.' She flew at him and hugged him. 'Pat's just the one for you.'

Richard beamed. 'Glad you approve.'

Kitty released him and stood back. 'When are you planning to be married?'

'Well, naturally, we'd like it to be next week.'

'Next week! You can't.'

'Actually, not as soon as that. We have to find somewhere to live. And you and the boys will need to find another bod to take my place, I guess.'

'Well, for a minute, I thought it might mean *we* would be turfed out.'

'What an idea! Andy and Des were here first, remember? Anyway, we don't want to take on a great barn like this, and considering we'll both be working, Pat thought a small, convenient, modern flat would suit us better.'

'Yes, of course it would. Do you know of anyone who would fit in here?'

'Andy has someone in mind, I think. He did mention a while ago that he had a friend who was wanting to share a flat. Of course this friend may have found something else by now.'

'Male or female?'

Richard looked surprised. 'I presumed a male, but I suppose it could be a girl.'

'Well, whoever it is, I'd like to be consulted. I have to live here, too.' Then a thought struck her. 'On the other hand, I don't think I fancy flatting with men without you here, Richard.'

'You can take care of yourself, or you're not my sister.'

'But it might cause talk.'

'Mixed flatting is prevalent, as you must know.'

'Of course I know, but it's not to say I entirely approve.'

'That's my old-fashioned sister. Well,

tell Andy you have a girl friend who'd like to move in.'

'I might do just that. But I can't think of anyone suitable just at the moment.'

TWELVE

Richard went out with Pat that evening, and Des had some project on, but Andy was home, and Kitty broached to him the subject of a flat mate when Richard moved out.

'Have you anyone in mind, Andy?'

'I've been sorting out in my mind a few chaps I know, but one has to be careful. They might seem all right, but one is never sure until having to live with them, and then it's awkward, if they don't pull their weight, to tell them to go.'

'Why not a tentative arrangement—say a trial for three months and then, if either party isn't happy, they agree to find somewhere else,' suggested Kitty.

'That sounds ideal, if it works. Anyway, we can all think about it, and you might come up with someone yourself. How about that doctor friend of yours?' Andy grinned as he added, 'I think that's a brilliant idea—free medical advice right on the premises.'

Kitty felt herself blushing. 'I wouldn't suggest it to him. Anyway, some of the time he's on night duty, and has to be on call at the hospital, so I guess he'd prefer his present quarters.'

Dr. Gregory, apparently recovering from his 'flu, didn't appear in the cafeteria for a couple of days, and Kitty hoped his cold hadn't developed into something worse.

She was busily engaged in clearing the tables after lunch when someone caught her around the waist from behind.

'None of that,' she said as she wrenched herself away.

'Don't be like that,' said Ian.

Kitty turned at the sound of his voice. 'Oh, it's you! I thought it was that cheeky Dr. Van Dorran. He was last one out, and I thought for a moment he'd returned.'

'Van Dorran? Would you like me to sort him out for you?'

'I can deal with him. I'm not exactly helpless. I had a course in judo once.'

'You're full of surprises. I never know what you're going to come out with next.'

'Have you recovered from your cold?'

'Yes, thanks. Back to normal.'

'Then what I'm going to say next is, are you needing a meal?'

'Am I ever! Only had time for a cup of coffee when I got up, and for breakfast, I munched an apple on my way to Casualty.'

'Take a seat and I'll bring you a tray.'

Kitty whisked off to the kitchen. Mrs. Hoddy had gone off to have what she called her afternoon snooze, and a couple of the kitchen maids were busy with the dishes.

Kitty heated up some Scotch broth, set a tray and carried it out to Ian. She set the steaming bowl before him. 'That's to be going on with. I'm afraid all that's left for second course is corned beef, or ham and salad. I'll fry you up some left-over mashed potatoes if you like.'

Ian picked up his spoon ready to begin on the soup. 'I like,' he said.

When she'd produced the second course, Kitty asked, 'Would you care for dessert? There's some stewed apricots and apples.'

'Just a cup of coffee is all I have time for,' said Ian, consulting his wrist watch.

When he'd finished, he took his tray to the counter, where Kitty and Doreen were wiping down.

'I'm a new man. Thanks very much. Must dash.' He was gone in a flash.

'Always in a hurry, these doctors,' said Doreen. 'Wouldn't be married to one of them for anything. You'd come a poor second to their precious patients.'

'Have you a boy friend at the moment?' asked Kitty.

'Well, sort of. Name of Wayne Bridges. I don't think I'll stick with him, though. He belongs to a motorbike gang, and his precious motorbike means more to him than any girl. Just like your Dr. Gregory and his patients.'

'*My* Dr. Gregory?' said Kitty, assuming surprise.

'I saw you fussing around him after lunch today. I was just coming in from the kitchen when he put his arm around you. So I made myself scarce.'

'Oh, he didn't mean anything,' said Kitty lightly.

When Kitty was going home that afternoon, she saw Dr. Gregory waiting at the gate.

'Hello,' he said as she approached. 'How about you and I going out to dinner? I really do owe you a meal after all the trouble I've landed you in.'

'What trouble?'

'Well, it was rather catastrophic when my car broke down the other evening.'

Kitty laughed. 'I think you came off worst. You were the one who caught the cold. Has your car been fixed?'

'No, not yet, but I've got a temporary

replacement loaned to me by the garage. It's just across the street.'

'It's rather early for dinner, and I'll have to go home and change and also leave something for the boys.'

'We've plenty of time for that. It's only four now. I've got the whole evening off. I'll run you home and then, when you're ready, we can take a drive before dinner. It's such a perfect day, I don't think a thunderstorm will dare to appear.'

Back at the house, Kitty hastily examined the contents of the fridge. 'Oh, good. There's enough steak casserole for the boys. Richard has a phenomenal appetite, and him as thin as a rake.'

'Some people burn it up in energy.'

'Yes, that's Rich. Always on the go.' As she talked, Kitty peeled potatoes, washed brussels sprouts, put out a tin of fruit salad where it could be seen, then wrote a note for Richard telling him she would be dining out.

'Where are we going for dinner, by the

way?' Kitty asked Ian as she propped up the note against the coffee pot where Richard would be sure to see it.

'I've just had an idea,' said Ian. 'How about going to the Moana Pool? The restaurant there is very good, I believe, and we could have a swim before dinner? You do have some swimming togs?'

'Of course I have. Oh, Ian, that would be lovely. You couldn't have thought of anything I'd enjoy more. I'll go and change now and collect my gear.'

She came out fifteen minutes later, looking fresh and pretty in a primrose polo-necked top, an elegantly cut pair of green slacks and carrying a short, mohair coat, all of which she had bought in her palmier days when she was working for Chester and Wearman.

She saw Ian through the kitchen window, strolling around the lawn looking at the plants, and went to join him.

'Should I have put on a dinner dress?' she asked.

Ian looked her up and down. 'You'll be the best dressed and loveliest one there.' He took her arm companionably. 'Let's get going, h-mmm? I'll have to drop by the hospital and pick up my own togs. It won't take long. Where are yours?'

'In a zip bag in the kitchen. I'll pick them up as we go through.'

Soon they were in Queen's Drive with its native bush bordering the roadway and a succession of panoramic views whose splendour was breathtaking.

Reaching Moana Pool and its surroundings, Ian parked the car, and they went their way to the changing rooms.

The water in the pool was a relaxing eighty degrees and they swam lazily together, pleased that the baths were not over-crowded as yet.

'This is marvellous,' said Ian as they reached the shallow end and paused for breath.

'Nothing like a warm bath to relax the

tensions, and I guess you get plenty of those,' said Kitty.

'Yes, Casualty requires quick action most of the time. Still, I find it challenging.'

'Have you considered general practice?'

'I'd like that eventually.'

'I imagine specializing would be more lucrative, wouldn't it?'

'I guess so. Take skin specialists—no night calls, usually nothing urgent. But consider the dullness of dealing with boils, adolescent acne and such. No, I prefer the variety of a G.P.'s life, even if it is mostly 'flu, babies, backaches and measles. There's always the necessity of keeping alert enough to spot the dangerous symptoms and to do something about it. Come on, let's do another two lengths and then we'll take ourselves to the restaurant before it fills up.'

They set off at a cracking pace, but Kitty found herself lagging on the second lap, and Ian adjusted his pace to hers.

They were both starving when they

finally emerged from the pool, and separated to get dressed.

Facing each other across a table, later, they grinned contentedly. 'I don't know when I've enjoyed myself so much,' said Ian.

'It was super.'

Studying the menu, Ian said, 'I'm so hungry I could eat an elephant.'

'*If* you could penetrate its skin with a knife and fork.'

'Let's put a couple of large steaks to the test, h-mmm? Or would you prefer roast beef or chicken?'

'I'd like roast beef with Yorkshire pudding. I cook lots of steak for the boys.'

'I'll have the same,' said Ian.

After the meal, feeling delightfully replete, they lingered over coffee in the lounge, chatting together as if they had known each other for years.

Kitty at last consulted her watch. 'Just look at the time. We'll be thrown out of here if we don't move soon and head for home. And neither of us will be fit for work tomorrow if we're out too late.'

'Yes, we must go—reluctantly for me. I'd like tonight to go on for ever.'

'The good times never do, though,' sighed Kitty.

'Why not? It's not like you to be a pessimist.'

'I guess I was just thinking back to when I was out of a job. I never dreamed such a thing could happen to *me*. Perhaps I was over-confident. It's not enough, these days, to be skilled and conscientious. One needs to have Lady Luck on one's side.'

'As far as *I'm* concerned,' said Ian, glancing at her sideways, 'it was a stroke of luck when you came to work in the cafeteria. We'd never have met, otherwise.'

Kitty felt a warm glow flow through her. She gave Ian a dreamy smile and their glances held for a long, breathless moment.

'No, we wouldn't, would we?' Kitty rose

to her feet. 'Richard will be sending out a search party for me if I'm not home soon.'

Kitty woke slowly the next morning, reluctant to allow the new day to intrude on her dreams. Before complete consciousness took over, she was aware of a feeling of blissful elation. As she became alert she knew, without doubt that she had fallen in love with Dr. Ian Gregory, irrevocably and completely.

For a minute or two she allowed this enchantment to remain unalloyed, and then a niggling doubt crept in.

What if, in spite of his flattering attentions, Ian wasn't at all serious about her? What if he just needed a companion for an occasional evening out? What if he intended to stay unattached until he was ready to launch himself into general practice?

What a fool she had been to be carried away by a few invitations from a personable doctor.

She would have to cool it. But how? Once in love, it was not the easiest thing in the world to turn that love off, like a flowing tap. It was going to be the hardest, darned thing she'd attempted.

THIRTEEN

Kitty went to work that morning, living for the moment when she would see Ian again. Perhaps she would be able to tell, just by the look in his eyes, if he were truly in love with her, as she was with him.

But he didn't put in an appearance for morning tea, nor lunch, nor afternoon tea. Should she drop him a note? Something short and friendly? Surely that would be the polite thing to do. Of course, she'd thanked him when he'd said goodnight at the house, and it might be overdoing it to write a note as well, making the whole thing more important than was intended. She waffled around, deciding in the end to wait until she saw Ian again. Which shouldn't be too long.

It was peculiar, though, that he hadn't

turned up at the cafeteria for at least *one* snack. He couldn't have been as eager to see her as she was to see him. Perhaps he was back pedalling, regretting the fact that he'd said some flattering remarks to a mere cafeteria hand.

By the time she arrived home that afternoon, Kitty's euphoric mood had changed to one of gloom. She began to prepare dinner in a lethargic way, listening all the time for the phone to ring. But not a tingle did it give forth.

After dinner Richard, who was reading the evening paper, said, 'I say, Kit, is your doctor friend involved in this helicopter rescue thing?'

'What rescue, exactly? There's always someone getting lost in the bush or the mountains.' She looked at the paper over his shoulder. 'Whereabouts is it?'

'Somewhere near the Knobby Range. Two climbers.'

Kitty felt her heart turn over. It would have to be Ian who accompanied the rescue team. He was the one on accident duty. 'Oh God,' she prayed silently, 'keep him safe.'

She listened anxiously every time the news came on the radio and, at ten-thirty, it was announced that a rescue had been made. The two climbers had been found—one with a broken leg and the other with head injuries. Both had fallen over a cliff, having been roped together. They had been flown back and were now in hospital, resting comfortably.

'Why do they always say the patient is comfortable?' commented Kitty. 'I bet one has a bad headache and the other is getting his leg put in plaster. What's comfortable about that?'

'They're probably under sedation,' said Richard. 'No need to get het up about it. Oh, *I* understand.' He gave her a shrewd grin. 'You were worried that Dr. Gregory was in danger, and now you know everything's all right, you're letting off steam to relieve your feelings. Am I right?'

'I guess so,' admitted Kitty, adding defensively. '*Anyone* would be anxious if someone they knew was involved in one of those hazardous rescue operations.'

Mrs. Hoddy was in a bad mood when Kitty arrived at the hospital the next morning. One of the kitchen staff had not turned up and she was shorthanded.

'She might have let me know,' she grumbled to Kitty. 'There's always one or the other of them away because they don't feel well. My guess is that they've had a late night and can't be bothered getting up, not even to pick up a phone and give me the news that they're not coming in.'

'I'll give you a hand with the vegetables,' offered Kitty.

'You've your own work to do.'

'I'll be as quick as I can with the sandwiches.'

'Well, don't skimp the fillings just because you're in a hurry,' cautioned Mrs. Hoddy. 'I like them done properly.'

'What's eating her?' whispered Doreen when Kitty joined her at the table to help with the sandwiches.

'I only offered to help with the vegetables, but I wish I'd kept quiet,' Kitty whispered back. 'She's short of a kitchen maid.'

They soon found out that the reason for Mrs. Hoddy's shortness of temper was caused by something more serious than staff problems.

After the morning tea rush, Mrs. Hoddy suddenly sat down and said with deep despair, 'I can't go on.'

Kitty, who'd just come into the kitchen with a tray of dishes, put them down on the sink bench and hurried over to her. 'What's wrong, Mrs. Hoddy?'

'It's this pain.' Mrs. Hoddy put her hand gingerly on her midriff. 'I've been getting it on and off for months, mostly during the night, but it's something fierce right now.'

'I'll get a doctor,' said Kitty and, not

heeding Mrs. Hoddy's feeble protest, rushed through to the cafeteria, hoping to find one of the doctors lingering over morning tea.

There was one, a tall, lanky young man with ginger hair who was tiredly drinking a cup of coffee. Kitty hastened up to him.

'Excuse me, Doctor, but Cook seems to be ill. Could you take a look at her?'

'Old Hoddy? Right. Where is she? In the kitchen?'

'Yes.'

He sprang up, and Kitty followed him back to the kitchen. Mrs. Hoddy was still sitting at the table, her head in her hands.

When the doctor had asked her several questions and prodded her gently but firmly in the painful area, he called for two orderlies to take her to one of the wards for observation.

Mrs. Hoddy said, with a faint show of spirit, 'And who's going to get the dinner for you doctors?'

'We won't starve,' said the doctor.

It was strange to see the normally active Mrs. Hoddy being carried out on a stretcher.

'I could well have walked,' muttered Mrs. Hoddy, upset at the indignity of being carried out of her own kitchen under the eyes of the staring staff.

'What do we do now?' said Doreen.

The rest of the kitchen staff had gathered together and they looked at Kitty for suggestions.

'We can't possibly manage on our own,' said Rona Smithers.

'Well, it's not in our power to hire staff,' said Kitty. 'I'll ring Matron.'

Matron answered the phone with a brisk 'Yes?'

Kitty explained the situation.

'Very unfortunate. I'll ring the labour exchange right away. In the meantime, do the best you can with regard to lunches. I'll see if I can find one of the junior nurses to help out.'

The junior nurse, Alison Proctor, arrived

shortly. She was a bright, pert girl, looking as if she were capable of turning her hand to anything.

'I hope you won't think this is a come-down—working in the cafeteria,' said Kitty, smiling at her.

'It's a marvellous change—a rest from the everlasting bedpans,' said Alison. 'Now tell me what you want me to do.'

'You can help Doreen in the cafeteria serving the doctors with their lunches. She'll tell you what to do.' She beckoned to Doreen. 'Here's someone to help you—Alison Proctor.'

'Am I glad to have you,' said Doreen. 'I was wondering how I could manage on my own as Kitty seems to be expected to help with the cooking.'

'And *I'm* feeling a bit desperate about *that*,' said Kitty. 'I'm not used to cooking for a crowd. Six is my limit.'

The two of them went off and Kitty looked around for Rona Smithers.

'Could we work on this together?' she

asked Rona. 'You must know more about it than I do.'

'Mrs. Hoddy had today's menu all planned. She writes it down and leaves it on her desk.'

They bent their heads over the menu.

Rona read it out, 'Cold meat, salads, steak hot-pot and vegetables. That shouldn't be too difficult.'

The time flew by much too fast and Kitty and Rona only just managed to have the containers ready for serving in the cafeteria by mid-day.

By one-thirty the rush was over and Kitty, sitting tiredly at the kitchen table with a cup of tea, was embarrassed and surprised to see Matron appear in the doorway. She hastily stood to attention, hoping Matron would not think she was slacking on the job.

But Matron said as she approached, 'Thank you, Miss Willet for stepping into the breach. I asked one of the doctors if he had enjoyed his lunch, and he seemed surprised that Cook hadn't been in charge. He said it was as good as usual. Well done.'

'Thank you, Matron,' said Kitty, her tiredness dissipating and her spirits soaring. A little praise could do wonders to the ego.

At home that night, around eight, the phone rang. Richard answered it.

'It's for you, Kit. A bloke.'

In the hall, Kitty picked up the receiver. 'Hello?'

'Ian here. Kitty, are you all right?'

'Of course I am.'

'You weren't in the cafeteria today.'

'I was in the kitchen doing the cooking, believe it or not. Mrs. Hoddy had some sort of attack and was whisked off to one of the wards.'

'Good lord. I hadn't heard that. How did you cope?'

'*You* can be the judge of that. Are you suffering from indigestion or whatever?'

Ian laughed. 'I didn't notice any difference in the food. It was good.'

'Well, Mrs. Hoddy did have it organized, more or less. I just had to finish it off.'

'They were lucky having you to take over.'

'I didn't enjoy it exactly. I'm hoping Mrs. Hoddy will make a speedy recovery or else that they provide a substitute.'

'I guess they will.'

'Ian ...' Kitty hesitated, then said, 'I do admire the good work you did in that rescue operation. It must have been dangerous.'

'Not at all. The ones to admire are the crew members of the helicopter. My part was just routine.'

'Well, I was a little worried.'

'It gives me a nice, warm feeling to have someone worry about, me, but there was no need. Kitty, I'll have to go. There's a stretcher coming in.' He rang off abruptly as always when he was on duty in Casualty.

'Well, thought Kitty, mollified, he did think about her enough to ring her when he had a minute to spare. But what sort of life was it for a girl to have a man friend like Ian? One could never depend on having his uninterrupted attention for long. She felt like casting him off. Why should she waste her best years never knowing when a date would be cancelled?

She said as much to Pat Matson one evening when she came round for dinner and they were in the kitchen together.

Pat said, 'I wouldn't like the sort of life that Dr. Ian Gregory has to offer a girl friend, but then, it's not my decision, is it?'

'It hasn't come to a decision yet. He pays me quite a bit of attention—when he can spare the time.'

It was in this mood that she accepted an invitation from Andy to a dance.

'It's rock-n-roll,' said Andy. 'D'you think you'd enjoy it?'

'I don't know whether I can do that or not.'

'You'll soon learn. It should be fun.'

'I'll try anything once,' said Kitty.

The dance hall was not too crowded when they arrived, and Kitty soon got the hang of rock-n-roll. She suddenly felt young and free as she and Andy gyrated to the music. Kitty was agreeably surprised to note that the band was Neil Woodward's. He must be doing quite well.

'D'you mind if I speak to the band leader when there's an interval?' Kitty asked Andy.

'No, of course not. He was in that pop concert, wasn't he? You haven't fallen for him, by any chance?'

'Certainly not. He had a flat in the same block where I lived before I moved in with Richard.'

'Well, in that case ... I was about to get jealous.'

'Now, none of that. We're just friends, you and I.'

Andy grinned down at her. 'I might try to alter that ...'

They both approached the band at

interval time, and Neil greeted Kitty with enthusiasm.

'If it isn't my old girl friend,' he said. 'Kitty, you look radiant.'

Kitty drew Andy forward. 'Neil, this is a friend of my brother, Richard's, Andy Pearce. We all flat in the same house.'

'Well, that's nice,' said Neil. 'I was sorry when you left. Pat told me you'd had some trouble finding a job. Did you eventually get something?'

'Yes, I work at the hospital.'

'Oh, good.' Neil looked at his watch. 'Duty calls. Nice to see you here, Kitty. Perhaps you'll come again.'

'Perhaps.'

Kitty and Andy walked away. 'What's this about your being his old girl friend?' asked Andy.

'Girl friend! Neil hasn't time for such luxuries. With him it's music, music, music all the way.'

'If you can call it music,' said Andy.

'It's pleasant to dance to, at least. They

have a good rhythm.'

'My word, yes. At most dances they have amplified records. Saves money, I suppose, but not the same glamour as a real dance band—just one man and a record player, and the amplification is always too loud—an assault on the eardrums.'

'I like to see band members all dressed alike in something glamorous. Once it used to be black dress suits and white frilled shirts, but those bright satin outfits do give an air of festivity.'

When the dance was over and they were leaving the hall, a short, fair man smiled at Kitty as if he knew her. He was accompanied by a small, rosy-faced woman.

'Who was that?' asked Andy when they were out of earshot.

'I don't know. He looked vaguely familiar, so I suppose I must have met him somewhere.'

The fact of where she had met him was

brought to her notice the very next day.

A temporary cook had been installed, much to Kitty's relief, and she was back in her old job in the cafeteria.

As she filled cups at lunch-time, someone said, 'Did you enjoy the dance last night?'

She looked up and saw the short, fair man smiling at her. Of course, she remembered him now. He'd been in the cafeteria only a couple of times or so. He must be a new member of the staff.

'Yes, thank you,' she said, smiling back in return.

As she looked up to serve the next customer, her gaze met the glowering eyes of Dr. Ian Gregory.

'So that's where you were when I rang you last night,' he said, his voice low and indignant.

'Have you any objection?' asked Kitty icily.

'Well, if you like to flirt around, it's your business, I suppose.'

Kitty felt an urgent impulse, when he stalked off, to rush after him and explain that it was only Richard's flat-mate, Andy, whom he'd already met, and who was nothing more than a friend. At least as far as *she* was concerned. She hoped Ian's show of jealousy had been only a thing of the moment. Oh, men! she thought irritably, why did they have to be born jealous?

A little later, as Kitty was clearing the tables, Ian came in. He approached her with an apologetic smile.

'I'm sorry I was such a bear,' he said. 'I guess it was Richard you were with.'

So he thought she wasn't attractive enough to be asked out by anyone other than her brother.

'It wasn't Richard,' she said curtly.

'May I ask who my rival is?'

'The word "rival" doesn't come into it. Aren't we just friends?'

'You and I? You know you mean more to me than "just friends."'

221

Kitty melted. She raised her round, innocent eyes to his. 'Do I?' she asked softly.

'Kitty, if we weren't in a public place, I'd give you a good shaking and then a resounding kiss.'

'There's nobody here but Doreen, and I'm sure she would welcome viewing a romantic scene to brighten her day.'

'You tantalizing brat. Now, tell me, who were you out with last night?'

Kitty hummed a few bars of the old song, 'Who were you with last night,' then said, 'Well, if you must know, it was only Richard's friend, Andy. You've met him.'

'Oh, Andy Pearce? He's not after you, is he?'

'Well, if encouraged ...' teased Kitty.

'Just let me catch you at it. Must dash.' Ian went off in his usual brisk fashion, his mind now concentrated on his duties in Casualty.

When Kitty had finished her work that day, she went along the hospital corridors to the ward where Mrs. Hoddy was installed. She was in a side room by herself, and when Kitty per her head around the door, Mrs. Hoddy, who was sitting up in bed, gave her a welcoming smile.

'Come in, girl. You're just the one I want to see.'

'How are you?' asked Kitty, pulling up a chair beside the bed and seating herself on it.

'It's me gallbladder playing up. I've been getting these attacks quite a bit lately, but I thought it was indigestion. I've had X-rays and they showed up these stones, so I guess it means an op, bother it. That's something I can do without. Now tell me, how are you managing in the kitchen?'

'Quite well,' said Kitty. 'But they seem to expect me to do the cooking. You'd started on the dinners yesterday, so there wasn't a great deal for me to do. Anyway, I didn't hear any complaints from the doctors.'

'How did you get on today, then?'

'They managed to find a temporary cook, thank goodness.'

'Who is it?'

'A Miss Browne.'

'What's she like?'

'I haven't seen much of her as yet, so it's hard to tell. She seems pleasant enough.' Kitty noted the doubtful expression on Mrs. Hoddy's face and added hastily, 'She isn't as good a cook as you are, though.'

'Oh, well,' Mrs. Hoddy leaned back against the pillows, satisfied, 'I guess she hasn't had my experience. And how are all the doctors?'

'As rushed as ever.'

'That nice young Dr. Gregory came to see me early this afternoon. Now there's a good chap you should set your cap at. Real sincere he is. I appreciate him coming in to see an old body like me. Not many would have bothered.'

'Yes, he *is* nice,' said Kitty, trying to look unconcerned.

'He won't stay single long with all the nurses rolling their eyes at him. My, what it is to be young.'

'It isn't all it's cracked up to be. I think I'd sooner be middle-aged and settled, with no decisions to make. Out of the rat race and enjoying a life of peace and serenity.'

Mrs. Hoddy gave a grim smile. 'Troubles and decisions don't disappear with middle-age, my girl. In fact, they get worse. Who was that writer who said youth was wasted on the young?'

'Shaw, I think. But that was only one man's opinion.'

'Well, I certainly enjoyed myself when I was young,' said Mrs. Hoddy. 'You mightn't think it to look at me, but in my teens I was a right, comely young woman with lovely, long auburn hair—so long I could sit on it.'

Kitty regarded Mrs. Hoddy thinning, grey locks. 'Did you never cut it?'

'Yes. I had it all sheared off when the

shingle was in fashion.'

'I hope you kept it.'

'Yes, I've a long rope of it tucked away somewhere, but I hate to look at it—reminding me of how it's changed.'

Mrs. Hoddy closed her eyes, and Kitty realising she had talked enough, said goodbye and took her departure.

FOURTEEN

The new cook for the cafeteria, Miss Browne, was not as calm or as competent about the job as was Mrs. Hoddy. She flapped around the kitchen in low-heeled shoes, wrinkled stockings, her hair escaping from her white cap, and wisps of it drifting down over the collar of her starched overall. She was decidedly nervous, thought Kitty.

As Kitty went to fetch boiled eggs and lettuces for the sandwiches, Miss Browne, who was tipping steak mince into an enormous saucepan, hailed her.

'I've forgotten your name, Miss er ...'

'I'm called Kitty.'

'Well, Kitty, would you fetch me the ingredients that go in the mince, please.'

Kitty fetched salt, pepper, instant onions, and curry powder.

When she'd put them on the table, Miss Browne said, 'How does Mrs. Hoddy make this stuff?'

'Sometimes the curry and onions, and sometimes a packet or two of mixed vegetables.'

'I'll try the curry today,' said Miss Browne. 'How much do you think this lot needs?'

'I'm not sure. About a dessertspoonful I suppose.'

The curry was the only hot dish Miss Browne managed to make that day, and the doctors had to be satisfied with cold meat and salad for their second choice. They made no complaints, but when curry appeared on the menu for the third day, there were rumbling grumbles.

'Has Mrs. Hoddy lost her memory?' asked one young doctor as he surveyed the curry simmering in the container. 'Tell her from me that curry is a dish to be enjoyed in small doses—not day after day after day.'

'Don't blame Mrs. Hoddy,' said Kitty. 'She's in hospital having an operation. The new cook is only temporary.'

'Hey, I didn't know about Mrs. Hoddy.' He raised his eyes to heaven. 'May she have a speedy recovery.'

After lunch, Kitty approached Miss Browne with diffidence. It was an awful cheek for a mere cafeteria hand to suggest a change of menu to the cook.

'Like a cup of tea?' Kitty asked Miss Browne, who was sitting at the kitchen table, her chin resting on her hands, and her general air being one of dispiritedness.

'I'd be glad of it,' said Miss Browne.

Kitty brought two cups to the table and sat down opposite Miss Browne.

Kitty took a sip of the hot tea, then cleared her throat. 'Miss Browne, I've had a request from one of the doctors that he'd like a change from curry. Apparently it doesn't agree with him.'

'Oh, dear! Then perhaps I could omit the curry powder and give them plain mince.'

'I think they'd appreciate chops or steak or something like that,' ventured Kitty, relieved that Miss Browne hadn't taken umbrage.

When Miss Browne had drunk her tea, she said, 'I'd better tell you I'm not much of a cook. I'm afraid I told a bit of a fib when applying for this position, saying I'd had experience. The only experience I've had is doing the cooking at home for myself. You see, I'm actually an office worker. I'm very good with figures, but my firm closed down and I was made redundant.'

'That's exactly what happened to me,' said Kitty, her eyes full of sympathy.

'It's a nasty feeling, isn't it?'

'It surely is. Do you live alone, then?'

'Yes, and when I had my job, I used to get a hot dinner in a restaurant most days, and at the weekends I made do with omelettes or fish.'

'I think the doctors would like fish for a change.'

'I'll have to confess that I bought mine already cooked from the fish shop. There's a very good one near my flat.'

'I'll help you make fish pies tomorrow, that is, if you'd like me too.'

'I would that. You're a good girl, Kitty.'

Kitty arrived at work a little early the next day so that she could devote some time in giving Miss Browne a hand.

At lunch time, the fish pies, covered in buttered breadcrumbs, browned in the oven, were a great success, and there were no adverse comments about the food that day from the doctors.

Miss Browne was so pleased that she wanted to make fish pies the following day, too.

'Now we know what they like,' she said to Kitty, 'things will be much easier. What do you think?'

'I think, let them wait for their fish pies a few days, then they won't get tired of them.'

Miss Browne's face fell. 'Shall we go

back to mince again?'

'What about beef olives?'

'Do you know how to cook them?'

'Yes. They're a bit fiddly, but quite easy.'

'How do you know all this? You're so young.'

'I cooked for my brother and father for two years after my mother died. She was a good cook, and I tried to emulate her, but of course, I failed miserably at times. Fortunately, my two men were very patient with me.'

'But you're flatting now, aren't you?'

'Yes. With my brother. You see, my father got married again and his wife didn't want Richard and I around. Actually, we're sharing a big house with friends of Richard's. I do most of the cooking for them because I get home first, but they take their turns at the weekends, which suits me, as I can gallivant if I want to.'

'I suppose you've dozens of boy friends?'

'Not so's you'd notice,' said Kitty with

an unconscious sigh, thinking of Dr. Ian Gregory—the man in her life who came and went. And, at the moment, it seemed to be mostly 'went.'

Kitty called again on Mrs. Hoddy when she'd finished work for the day.

'They're operating on me tomorrow, first thing,' said Mrs. Hoddy.

'Are you nervous?' asked Kitty.

'Scared to death,' admitted Mrs. Hoddy with a wry smile.

'The pre-med will take care of the scared feeling, and just think, this time tomorrow, it will all be behind you and you'll be on the way to recovery. You can be sure they'll take extra good care of you, because you're an important person in this hospital.'

'You've cheered me up no end, and thanks for coming in.'

The anaesthetist tapped at the door and came in with a list of questions to be answered by Mrs. Hoddy, and Kitty took her departure.

Arriving home, she went into her usual rush of preparing dinner. Richard rang while she was in the middle of it to tell her he was bringing Pat for the meal.

'Oh dear, I don't think I've enough steak to go around,' said Kitty, 'but if you're prepared to have a smaller portion, bring her by all means. I'll put some extra potatoes and greens in the pots. But I do like to have more notice when you want to bring home a guest, Richard. Remember that in future.'

'Will do.' Richard sounded inordinately cheerful.

Richard and Pat were a little late in arriving, and Des was bemoaning the fact of having to wait for his dinner.

'We'll give them another five minutes and if they're not here by then, I'll give you yours,' offered Kitty. 'I'd hate to see you die of starvation.'

When Richard and Pat finally appeared, the news they announced banished all thought of food from their minds.

Pat extended her left hand. 'Look,' she said.

'You're engaged!' said Kitty, her gaze riveted on the modest diamond ring on Pat's finger. 'Oh, how lovely.'

'We're not going to wait too long before we get married, either,' said Richard. He put his arm possessively around Pat. 'Are we, m'love?'

Pat smiled fondly at him. 'What an impetuous suitor, to be sure. I guess we won't wait any longer than it takes to find us a house. We've decided to buy one. It will have to be modest, of course, but we've worked it out, and it will be cheaper than paying rent, even with rates and insurance and mortgages to pay, and at least it will be *ours.*'

'I think you're very sensible,' said Kitty, feeling a faint stab of jealousy. If only it were she and Ian who were looking for a house.

Then another thought occurred to her. If Richard moved out of this place, what would she, Kitty, do? Des had mentioned something about being moved to another school in a distant town, then there would be just her and Andy, and they wouldn't be able to afford the rent unless they found someone else to share.

She said to Richard when they were alone for a moment the next morning, 'Do you know of anyone who could take your place here when you and Pat get married?'

Richard, who was giving her a hand with the dishes, looked at her sharply. 'Are you worried you'll be homeless again?'

'Well, I guess I am.'

'It would be ideal if you and Andy could pair off.'

'Not for me, it wouldn't. I like Andy, but not for a husband.'

'There must be plenty of young folk looking for a good house to share.'

'The thing is to find the right person.'

'I guess so. But in the event of them not being to your liking, you could always give them the push.'

'I suppose so, but how does one say "please get out" in a tactful way?'

'That's easily done. You could invent a country cousin who's coming to live in the city and that you require the room for her.'

'I'm not in the habit of telling fibs,' said Kitty, giving him a haughty look. She could see that Richard was not unduly concerned about any future tenants of the house. But then, he wouldn't have to cope with them.

Richard hung up the tea-towel. 'Now, listen, Kit, you'll be getting married yourself one of these days, so take that worried look off your face. Anyhow, what about Ian? He seems keen on you.'

'*Seemed* keen. I don't see him very often now.'

'What happened? Did you have a row?'

'No. No row. Too many things come between us.'

'Such as? Other girls?'

'I don't *know* of any girls. It could

be that, but his excuse is always one thing—work.'

'Well, I suppose some chaps would make work an excuse if they wanted to cool off a romance, but I can't think Ian is like that. He doesn't seem the type to give his affections lightly.'

'One can't always go by first impressions,' said Kitty sadly.

Ian came in late at lunch-time that day.

'Could I have a word with you later?' he asked Kitty, as she handed him a cup of coffee.

'You may,' beamed Kitty, her grievances against Ian forgotten in her pleasure at seeing him again.

He made room for the coffee on his tray. He had a plate heaped with a couple of chops, three vegetables and two rolls on the side. He must have had a busy morning and in need of a more generous lunch than he usually had.

Fortunately, he was not called away

before he'd finished it, and he lingered in the dining-room until the other doctors had gone, then approached Kitty who had begun on the job of wiping down the tables.

'Sit down a minute,' he invited.

'I can't do that.'

'Why not?'

'We kitchen hands are not supposed to fraternise with the doctors,' said Kitty primly.

'What nonsense.'

'No, honestly. I know Doreen's watching me like a hawk. I can feel her eyes piercing my back.'

'It's nothing to do with her. She's not your boss.'

'She's a gossipy type. She might tell Mrs. Hoddy when she comes back. It would mean the sack for me.'

'Well, listen. My life has been one long round of over-time, urgent calls and what-have-you. It's so damned frustrating when one wishes to pursue a certain lady friend. Now, let's make a date, quick, before I'm called away.' He glanced at the loudspeaker on the wall. 'And don't you dare ring,' he threatened it.

'When are you free?' asked Kitty.

'Sunday—the whole day. Can we go out somewhere in the country or round the peninsular?'

'I'd like that. I'll pack a lunch.'

'You won't, you know. You do enough cooking as it is. We'll find a good restaurant.'

The speaker intoned, 'Calling Dr. Gregory, calling Dr. Gregory.'

Ian gave it a baleful glare. 'What did I tell you? I'm at that thing's mercy. I'll call for you tennish, Sunday?'

'I'll be ready,' said Kitty.

FIFTEEN

Kitty woke early on Sunday morning, and her first thought was of the day's outing with Ian. She threw back the bedclothes, put her feet on the floor and ran to the window, praying that the sky would be clear and sun shining.

The sun was sending its first rays over the hills, burnishing them with golden light, and the sky had a pearly translucence that boded well for a fine day.

It was too early to get up yet, so Kitty went back to bed to dream of the day ahead—if only nothing happened to prevent it. But once away from the hospital, Ian would be out of range of that tyrant, the loud-speaker.

At seven, she turned the radio on softly to hear the news, hoping there would be no reports of massive accidents. Saturday nights and the early hours of Sunday mornings were the worst times for accidents and sometimes it could mean that all leave was cancelled for the doctors in Casualty.

But the news reported nothing of any consequence as regarded accidents on the local scene, and Kitty got up at seven-thirty, went to the kitchen and made herself a cup of tea and a slice of toast.

It was the custom of the household that each member got his own breakfast at his own time on Sunday mornings, and the boys usually slept late.

Kitty busied herself making a green salad to leave for the boys' lunch. There was cold meat in the fridge and plenty of tins of fruit. They were used to managing without her and would probably enjoy being a male household for the day.

She was filled with a delightful sense of holiday spirit. No cooking to do! It was thoughtful of Ian to have remembered that she was normally involved in a lot of food preparation, and to give her a day free from it.

Promptly at ten Ian arrived. The morning had blossomed into a warm, sunny day, and Kitty had put on a green and white patterned print frock with a white cardigan thrown over her shoulders.

'I won't need a coat, will I?' she asked Ian when she had greeted him at the door.

'No. According to the weather report at seven, it will be fine all day.'

'Where are we going?' asked Kitty when she had settled into the seat beside Ian and they were moving through the suburbs.

'It's a surprise. I've got it all planned.' He looked down at her. 'You've no objections to surprises?'

Kitty smiled. 'I love them. Nice ones, of course.'

They took the harbourside drive along the Portobello Road and before long Ian turned the car into Glenfalloch woodland gardens, a lovely spot where the azaleas and rhododendrons were blooming in profusion.

'Morning-tea time,' said Ian. 'Have you been here before?'

'A couple of times on a bus ride.'

They went into the Chalet and did full justice to a generous morning tea, then walked through the gardens, dappled with shade from tall trees, staying for a moment to admire the peacocks on the green lawn, and were delighted when one of them displayed his tail in an iridescent fan.

'Are we here for the day?' asked Kitty.

'No, we're going a little further. It's such an ideal day for a Peninsula tour.'

Ian drove the car in a leisurely way so that both of them could enjoy to the full the varied scene opening before them—the sparkling waters and the rising hills clad in their fresh spring greenery.

Arriving at Portobello, they parked the car and took a brisk walk around the bay, working up an appetite for lunch. In the restaurant, they sat at a table for two, both of them smiling at each other in the sheer pleasure of being together.

Afterwards, they found a secluded spot where Ian spread the car rug and, with their backs propped against a huge tree, they talked and talked and talked, the words spilling out as they explored each other's minds and became better acquainted with their respective backgrounds.

Ian, it appeared, had a married sister living in Brisbane. His father, having developed arthritis, had persuaded his wife that the warmer climate would be kinder to his aches and pains, and so they had packed up and gone.

'M-mmm. I suppose Dunedin is rather cold,' commented Kitty.

'It's not too bad. The sea water tempers the cold. I love it. I find it bracing. Too much heat dulls the brain—well, *my* brain.'

'If you were working in hospitals over there,' said Kitty, 'you'd be in an air-conditioned atmosphere the same as here.'

'I guess so, but in off-duty hours here, one can get out and breathe clean, pure air.'

'I guess every place has its climatic drawbacks. I'd take off like a shot to a warm place—if I had the chance—when the snow is inches thick on the ground here. B-rrr! Don't let's think about it.'

'One of these days,' said Ian lightly, 'you and I might take a trip over there and find out how we like it.'

Kitty picked up a fallen twig and broke it into pieces. What, exactly, was Ian suggesting?

'I think it's time we were making for home,' she said, jumping up and walking towards the car.

Ian picked up the car rug, shook it and followed her to the car. He opened the passenger seat for her and got in his side. He looked sideways at her with a quizzical expression, then turned on the ignition and set the car in motion.

When they arrived at Kitty's house, she

said, 'Come along in for a snack. Unless you have another engagement?'

'No,' said Ian. 'I'm all yours.'

Kitty gave him a quick smile. 'I hope you like pizzas.'

'I do indeed.'

'Let's hope the boys haven't raided the fridge and eaten the lot.'

Richard and Pat were in the kitchen assembling a meal.

'What are you having?' asked Kitty.

Richard indicated a cheese and spaghetti pizza. 'We were just about to warm it up. There's another in the fridge. They're only small. We'll need both if you and Ian are here for tea.'

'We are,' said Kitty.

'Oh, good,' said Pat. 'I've brought a couple of French rolls a yard long. That should do us.'

When they'd had the meal, Kitty and Pat dealt with the dishes to the kitchen, chatting companionably about their respective day's outings.

'Rich and I had a long tramp,' said Pat. 'It was great, but I'm feeling a bit stiff.'

'I hope you haven't overdone it,' said Kitty. 'It's not that long since your operation.'

'I've forgotten all about *that*. An appendicectomy is nothing nowadays. I'm just pleasantly tired. Anyhow, we're not going out tonight. We've decided to stay here and watch the big film on telly.'

'Ian and I are in the same state—pleasantly tired. I think I'll suggest to him we do the same, that is, if you don't mind our company.'

Pat laughed gaily. 'Kitty, my love, it's *your* house—not mine. Are you sure you want to see that film, though?'

'*I* do. We'll see what Ian says.'

Ian was enthusiastic. 'It's not often I get to see a long film uninterruptedly.'

There were just the four of them home that evening, and they sat around the television set, the men with their legs stretched out, relaxed and at ease.

Kitty became absorbed in the film to the exclusion of all else, and was brought back to reality by a nudge from Pat who indicated the two men. Both were sound asleep.

'Typical,' whispered Pat.

'So much for the exhilarating company of their girl friends,' whispered Kitty with a smothered giggle.

Soon after that there was a burst of gunfire in the film and both Ian and Richard woke with a start.

'Did you enjoy the nap?' asked Pat.

'I haven't been asleep,' said Richard indignantly.

'Neither have I,' said Ian. 'I just closed my eyes for a moment to rest them.'

'Well, the film's over now,' said Pat. 'What was the plot?'

'All right, all right,' said Richard. 'I went to sleep, I admit. But blame the film makers. It's their job to keep us awake.'

'I agree,' said Ian. 'If they will keep producing these tired old plots, what can they expect?' He grinned ruefully. 'I'm sorry, girls. It was a most uncouth thing to do.'

'Not to worry,' said Kitty. 'I had difficulty in keeping awake myself near the end. It's all that fresh air we inhaled today. I'll put the kettle on and make some tea.'

'I'll help,' said Ian, rising with alacrity. 'I must atone for my sins somehow.'

In the kitchen he said as he assembled cups and saucers while Kitty buttered some crackers. 'Are you cross with me?'

'Whatever for? For doing a perfectly natural thing like dropping off to sleep during a film? Now, if I'd been in the middle of telling you some amusing story and you floated off, it would have been a different cup of tea.'

Ian came behind her and encircled her waist with his arms. 'Turn around,' he said.

Kitty turned and raised shining eyes to his, and Ian took this golden opportunity to kiss her with fervour.

'Ah, Kitty, you're the sweetest thing,' he said. He kissed her again.

The whistling kettle gave voice in a rising scream, and he said, 'Damn that thing,' and reached out a hand and turned it off.

'That's torn it,' said Kitty. 'Pat and Rich will now be expecting sustenance after that raucous announcement.'

She extracted herself from Ian's arms and made the tea, but her spine continued to tingle from the warm, delicious felicity engendered by Ian's kisses.

After supper, they sat around chatting until Ian said, 'Well, I suppose I'd better be going.' He rose to his feet and Kitty accompanied him to the door.

'Thank you for a wonderful day out,' she said.

'And thank *you* for coming with me and being such a delightful companion.' He put his arm around her. 'One for the road?' he asked, planting a firm kiss on her soft mouth.

He went off, and Kitty stood for a few moments watching his car until it disappeared, then looking dreamily at the frosty sky where a slender moon with an attendant star had risen above the dark outline of the hills.

Back inside, she collected the supper dishes and put them on a tray. 'I'll deal with these and be off to bed,' she said to Richard and Pat who were sitting holding hands in a state of dreamy bliss. 'Goodnight, you two.'

Pat roused herself. 'Want some help?'

'No. In fact, I forbid it.'

After she'd tidied up in the kitchen, Kitty ran herself a bath and soaked happily in the luxury of steaming, scented water, feeling the aches of the unaccustomed exercise of the day seep out of her bones.

In bed, she turned out the light and drowsed off to sleep with the thought of

Ian's warm kisses still glowing inside her.

He must be serious, she told herself, full of hope. But she wished she was as sure of him as Richard was of Pat.

SIXTEEN

Doreen greeted Kitty with the information, on Monday morning, that the kitchen staff had had a whip around, after Kitty had left on Friday, to buy some flowers for Mrs. Hoddy.

'We included you in,' said Doreen.

'Oh, good,' said Kitty. 'How much do I owe?'

'Fifty cents,' said Doreen. 'I took the flowers up to her and she was quite touched. I hope they have the effect of making her more amiable to the staff when she comes back.'

'How was she?' asked Kitty, handing over a fifty cent piece.

'Doing very well. She's been up and about.'

'I'll pop in and see her after work

tonight,' said Kitty.

But in the middle of the morning, when Doreen and Kitty were hard at it making sandwiches, Mrs. Hoddy came in wearing a scarlet dressing-gown over a purple-flowered nightgown, and pink slippers on her feet.

'Mrs. Hoddy!' said Kitty, jumping up. 'Whatever are you doing here?'

'Just making sure you're all keeping your work up to scratch.' She looked around in a proprietory way, her gaze critical.

Miss Browne and Rona Smithers stared at Mrs. Hoddy with apprehension as that lady approached them.

'You're my stand-in, I presume,' she said to Miss Browne, eyeing her up and down and not missing the shapeless, flat shoes, the wispy hair and the starched apron which was crumpled and spotted with raw egg.

'I hope you're feeling better, Mrs. Hoddy,' said Miss Browne stiffly, looking like a petrified rabbit.

'Not so's you'd notice,' said Mrs. Hoddy morosely. She went to the cutlery drawer, took out a spoon and dipped it into the stew that Miss Browne had simmering on the stove. She tasted the mixture, made a face and said, 'Hmmm, a bit tasteless. It needs more salt and some soya sauce to give it some pep. It's time I was back here.' She gave Miss Browne a withering look.

'I do my best,' said Miss Browne. 'No one could do more than that.'

'I daresay. But to my mind it's best to know something about a job before taking it on.'

Miss Browne's mouth took on an obstinate line. 'The doctors don't complain.'

'Mrs. Hoddy,' said Kitty, sensing a first-class row brewing. 'You shouldn't be on your feet. Sit down and I'll make you a cup of tea.'

'Thanks, me girl, but I'd better be getting back to the ward before they send out a search party for me. I'm hoping to be home in a couple of days and then I'm to recuperate for three weeks before I start work.' She lowered her voice. 'Walk with me to the door.'

Just outside the kitchen door she turned to Kitty and said, 'That woman! What's she doing in my kitchen? She's not even clean. Couldn't they get someone better than that?'

'She's quite clean, really,' said Kitty. 'I know she doesn't look tidy and neat like you, but she's used to office work, sitting at a desk, and she finds standing up most of the day rather hard on her feet, hence those old, flat shoes. She does wear a clean apron every day, but she gets flustered and now and again spatters things. When she arrives in the mornings in her good clothes, she's quite smart.'

'It's hard to believe. Nevertheless, I can't wait to get back to my kitchen. It's plain boring lying in bed doing nothing.'

Mrs. Hoddy ambled away and Kitty

went into the kitchen.

Miss Browne said to her, 'Mrs. Hoddy shouldn't start work too soon, although I could see she was itching to get back. Operations are tricky things, especially at her age. She could get a set-back. Anyway,' she added, her own future uppermost in her mind, 'what on earth am *I* going to do?'

'Perhaps you could get a job somewhere else in the hospital,' suggested Kitty.

'I'd do anything, anything.'

'Even if you don't land a job, there's always the dole,' said Kitty.

'Oh, I couldn't, I just couldn't. The disgrace.'

'It's no disgrace, but I do know how you feel. I was pretty near to going on it myself a few weeks back.'

It wasn't long after this that Kitty had a ring from her former employer, Mr. Chester, one evening.

'I'm starting up in business on my own in about a month,' he told her, 'and I wondered if you'd be interested in working in my office. It would be just a small place to start with, but I hope to work it up to bigger things. How about it?'

Kitty was about to joyfully assent, but hesitated, overcome by the knowledge that for some odd reason, she had no wish to work in an office again. She *liked* it in the cafeteria—the bustle, the comings and goings, the banter of the doctors. But the real reason was perfectly plain. She would not have the chance of seeing Dr. Ian Gregory so often.

Not that the brief encounters at morning tea and lunchtime were significant, except for the fact that, if she didn't see Ian at least once in the day, that day was dull indeed. Then an idea struck her.

'Mr. Chester,' she said into the phone, 'I'm flattered you thought of me, but I'm afraid I can't leave my present job at the moment.'

'But the job you've got at the hospital

isn't important, is it?'

'We're short staffed, and I really am needed at present. But listen, I do know of someone—a Miss Browne. She's older than I am, and experienced in office work. She's a very obliging person and I'm sure she would suit you.'

'Very well, if I can't persuade you to work for me, I may as well try her out. Tell her to come and see me.'

The next day, when Kitty passed on the news, Miss Browne was overjoyed. 'Kitty, I can't thank you enough,' she said, her chin trembling with emotion. 'But are you sure I'm not too old? He's used to a young thing like you.'

'Of course you're not too old. He'll be much better off with someone capable and experienced like you. Why don't you ring him up now and make an appointment to see him?'

'Perhaps I could. But I can't leave here with all the dinners to cook.'

'You're entitled to an hour off after

lunch. Make it for then. Strike while the iron's hot.'

'Yes. Yes, I will.' Miss Browne went to the phone and rang Mr. Chester, having got his number from Kitty. She was away for ten minutes, and came back, her cheeks flushed and her eyes bright.

'He'll see me,' she said. 'He sounded so nice over the phone—a real gentleman, the sort I'm used to working for.'

'Well, good luck,' said Kitty.

Ian came in late for lunch that day. He rushed up to the counter which, fortunately, had no one there but Kitty.

'I've had some bad news,' he told her.

Kitty looked at him in consternation.

Ian went on, 'I've had a cable that my father has had a stroke. I've made arrangements to fly over to Australia and I'm leaving at two this afternoon.'

'Oh, Ian, I'm sorry. I hope you won't find him too bad.'

'I hope not. People do recover from strokes, but it must be serious for them to have sent for me.'

'Have you time for coffee and sandwiches?'

'No, I'll get something to eat on the plane. I've only to throw a few clothes into a suitcase. That won't take me long.' He took her hands in his and gave them a squeeze. 'Look after yourself,' he said, and turned and hurried away.

Kitty felt as if a great gap had come into her days, without the expectation of seeing Ian at least once in the twenty-four hours, even if she didn't actually talk to him.

Mrs. Hoddy returned to the cafeteria two or three days later against her doctor's orders.

'I'll go mad if I stay at home,' she said to Kitty. 'I'll just take over the simple jobs that I can sit down to—the sandwiches, for instance, and I can supervise you and Doreen. Miss Browne I don't know about.'

'She's already been to see Matron about

it, as she was hired on a temporary basis only, and she has also found another job more suited to her abilities—office work.'

'Oh! Well, she might have consulted *me.*' Mrs. Hoddy looked taken aback.

'She doesn't start this other job for a week or two, so I guess she wouldn't mind staying on here in the meantime to give you a hand until you're feeling stronger. Why don't you ask her?'

'I might do that. Where is she?'

'I think she's helping with the vegetables.'

'Well, tell her I want a word with her.'

Kitty went over to the bench where Miss Browne was scraping carrots.

'Mrs. Hoddy wants to talk to you,' she said.

'Have I done anything wrong?'

'No, of course not. I told her about your new job, and I think she wants you to stay here until you start. Oh, Miss Browne, I'm so glad you liked Mr. Chester. I thought you would. I know you'll be happy working for him.'

Miss Browne beamed. 'Yes. I felt I had found my rightful niche. And all thanks to you, Kitty.' She washed her hands and went over to Mrs. Hoddy and, as Kitty went into the cafeteria, she saw them chatting together quite amicably.

Kitty was glad to have Mrs. Hoddy back at work, even though at times she was inclined to be crotchety, which condition was only to be expected after so recent an illness. Although she wasn't her usual brisk self, she took the reins of managing the cafeteria into her capable hands, and the menus consequently improved, much to the satisfaction of the doctors. They decided to show their appreciation of her services by clubbing together and buying her a set of pottery coffee mugs for her home.

When, on behalf of them all, two of the doctors came into the kitchen and presented the parcel to her, Mrs. Hoddy was at first flabbergasted into silence, and then burst into tears.

'Now, now, Mrs. Hoddy,' said young Dr. Grey. 'Don't you like them, then?'

'They're beautiful! It's only from being weak from me illness that I can't help letting these silly tears fall.' Mrs. Hoddy mopped her eyes and gave them a feeble smile. 'I guess I'm overcome with your kindness.'

The other doctor patted her shoulder. 'You must take care and not overdo it, Mrs. Hoddy. We can't do without you.'

When they'd gone, Mrs. Hoddy said to Kitty, who had been an interested onlooker, 'Well, now, wasn't that good of them? These mugs will come in handy when my family visit me. They drink nothing but coffee. Me, I can't go past a good cup of tea.'

The present from the doctors put new life into Mrs. Hoddy, their show of appreciation doing much to boost her ego, and she began to return to normal health much faster than most patients.

Meanwhile, Kitty waited eagerly each day to hear from Ian. He would find the time to send her an aerogram, surely. But, by the next weekend, when she had had no word, she decided he must be one of those people who abhor writing letters. Or else the worst had happened, and he was engulfed in funeral arrangements for his father.

Saturday was one of those mornings, bright, beautiful and crisp, which enticed one to be out and about, enjoying the warm sunshine.

Richard and Andy remarked at breakfast that such a day was too good to waste doing chores about the house, so how about a day climbing the hills?

'I'll ring Pat,' said Richard, 'and then we'll assemble some lunch and take off to the wilds.'

'What about your doctor friend?' Andy asked Kitty as Richard went to the phone.

'He's in Australia. His father is very ill.'

'Well, never mind. I'll quite enjoy having you to myself.'

'It's a foursome, Andy, and we'll stick together if you don't mind. Too many people get lost in mountains by separating.'

'As if I didn't know,' said Andy with a grin.

Kitty set about preparing a picnic lunch with the help of Andy, while Richard rushed about, making beds and tidying up. He then went off to pick up Pat.

Pat brought a neat packet of sandwiches and a flask of coffee, and they packed the food, together with another flask of coffee into two haversacks.

An hour's ride in Richard's car brought them to the Rock and Pillar Range, where they parked and locked the car. Richard and Andy each humped a pack on their backs, and they set off.

It was a splendid way to spend the day, thought Kitty as she walked along the narrow track with a spring in her feet, enjoying the scenery and especially the intoxicating freshness of the air. No smog here. Why did people love to live in towns where they were jostled and pushed in busy streets, and breathed in air tainted by industrial smoke?

The only thing missing in this paradise was the presence of Ian. Perhaps there would be a letter from him when she returned home, to tell her he was thinking of her as she was of him. In her mind's eye, she saw him in the bosom of his family and it occurred to her that the last person he would have in mind would be Kitty, the cafeteria dogsbody.

At some steep bits, she allowed Andy to take her hand and pull her along. His clasp was warm and friendly and, although Andy squeezed her hand affectionately, she felt no tingling of the senses.

When they had walked for an hour, they came to a flat, green piece of ground and decided to have lunch. Andy had brought a light rug and they spread this on the ground, brought out the sandwiches and flasks of coffee and sprawled themselves on the rug, eating with appetite the sandwiches and thirstily drinking the coffee as though it were nectar of the gods. They finished off their simple meal with apples and bananas.

'This is what we should do *every* weekend,' said Pat. 'Recharge our batteries with good mountain air. It would set us up no end. Who agrees?'

'We all do, I guess,' said Kitty. 'But things come up ...'

'Such as a certain fascinating doctor who shall be nameless,' teased Andy.

They were reluctant to leave, but it was imperative to be back in civilisation before darkness fell, or they would indeed be in trouble.

They packed the empty flasks and the plastic mugs and began to walk briskly across the grass to the track. They hadn't got out of the clearing when there was a cry from Kitty, who was bringing up the rear. The others stopped and turned round to see her lying on the grass.

'Hey, help me up, someone,' she called cheerfully. 'I've fallen in such an awkward way, I can't seem to find my feet.'

Richard and Andy dropped their packs and held out helping hands. They hoisted her to her feet.

Richard said, 'How did you manage to fall? There's nothing to fall over.'

'Oh, yes there is,' said Kitty. 'It was a large stone half buried in the grass.'

Andy found the stone. 'Yes, here it is. The top's quite sharp. No wonder it tripped you up.'

'Well, we'd better get going,' said Richard.

Pat noticed Kitty's contorted face as she put her weight on her foot. 'You've twisted your ankle, haven't you?' she said.

'I'm afraid so. The pain's excruciating. Just let me rest it a minute. I'm sure it will soon get better.'

'I think you had better sit down for a while,' said Andy, undoing his pack and bringing out the rug.

'I'll take a look at it,' said Pat.

Kitty was thankful when they lowered her to the ground. Pat unlaced Kitty's sturdy walking shoe and eased it off, then felt gently around the ankle. 'It's swelling up fast, I'm afraid. It's either a break or a strain.' She looked up at Richard. 'Have you a bandage in your pack?'

'Yes. I've got a small first-aid kit. Never go on a tramp without it, but this is the first time it's been called for.' He rummaged around and brought out the packet. 'This do?'

'I'll need a crepe bandage,' said Pat, opening the cardboard box. 'Yes, there's one here.' She turned to Kitty. 'I'd better peel off your sock.' She rolled up the leg of Kitty's slacks and eased off the thick sock. Then she tore off the cellophane wrapping from the bandage and began to wind it firmly around Kitty's ankle, finally fixing it with a small safety-pin.

'That feels better,' said Kitty, glad of the support of the bandage.

'I'm afraid you won't be able to put your shoe back on,' said Pat, 'but at least I can put your sock over the bandage.'

Pat did this as gently as she could, but Kitty had to grit her teeth to stop herself crying out in pain.

Richard put her shoe in his haversack and the three of them stood around looking at her in dismay.

'Well, hoist me up,' said Kitty, 'I think I can manage to walk.'

Once on her feet, she tried to walk, but the pain overwhelmed her and she had to stop.

'I'm sorry,' she said, 'I'm afraid I just can't do that walk. Whatever shall we do? It's impossible for you boys to carry me over the steep bits.'

Richard said, 'Let's sit down and plan what to do.'

'It's obvious to me,' said Pat, 'that we need help. It's too dangerous to try to carry her out without a stretcher of some sort. I think you two boys should hot-foot it back to the car and then to the nearest phone and ring the hospital. They'll probably send a helicopter. If we stay here on this open patch of ground, we should easily be seen, and the 'copter could even land, I imagine.'

'Yes, I think that's the best idea,' said Andy.' He looked at his watch. 'If we hurry, we should be able to organize things before dark. But if we can't, what about it then?'

Richard said, 'We'll leave our packs. There's about a cup of coffee left and a sandwich or two, and our oilskins. We can move faster without the haversacks.'

'Do be careful,' cautioned Pat. 'Watch every step you take.'

Kitty said, 'This is ridiculous. All this fuss about a twisted ankle. What is the helicopter crew going to say when they find out what a trivial thing they've been called out for?'

'Well, try and walk,' said Richard with cool logic.

'Help me up, then.'

Richard heaved her to her feet, still holding her by the shoulders, waited for her to move. Kitty put her weight gingerly on the swollen foot. The pain made her flinch, but she doggedly tried again and let out a yelp of anguish.

'Are you satisfied?' asked Richard as he lowered her to the ground. 'I'm sorry, old girl. I know how painful a sprained ankle can be, having had one myself many years ago.'

'We'd better not waste too much time,' said Andy, looking at his watch.

'No,' said Pat. 'We don't want to spend the night here.'

'I don't want to alarm you,' said Andy, 'but don't eat all the food at once, just in case we're longer than we think.'

'If the worst comes to the worst,' said

Pat, 'I'll scout around for some bracken to lie on, and the oilskin and the rug should keep out the cold. Now do get started. The sooner you ring the hospital, the sooner we'll have help.'

SEVENTEEN

When the boys had gone, Pat said, 'Would you like some coffee now, Kitty, just to ward off shock?'

'No, it's not long since we had some. We'd better conserve what supplies we have.'

'You're not inferring that we'll be here for days, are you?'

'I hope not. The thing is, they might have difficulty in seeing us, but I suppose the boys know approximately where we are.'

'The thing to do would be to rig up some sort of hoist.' Pat looked around and her gaze lighted on Kitty's red scarf. 'What say I climb the highest tree and tie the scarf on top?'

'I wouldn't do that,' said Kitty. 'You

might fall, and then there would be two accident cases.'

'The obvious thing is to light a fire and put on plenty of green stuff to make smoke.'

'Neither of us smoke, so what about matches?'

'Richard probably has a box in his haversack.'

'Of course!' Kitty said. 'He doesn't smoke either, but he'd always be prepared with matches on a hike like this, even though we had the thermos flasks.'

Pat was searching in Richard's haversack. 'Eureka! I've found a full box.'

Pat began to scout around for twigs and soon had a pile of them. 'What time should we light the fire?' she asked Kitty.

'Oh, not yet. The boys will hardly be out of the bush yet. I'd say about four.'

Pat continued to search for firewood and, coming back with an armful, fell flat on her face.

Kitty, forgetting for a moment her

injured foot, half rose to her feet. She cried out in pain, sank to the ground and a blackness descended on her.

Later, she became aware of a dampness on her head, and opened her eyes to see Pat's anxious face bending over her as she bathed Kitty's forehead with a damp handkerchief.

'Thank goodness you've come to your senses. You fainted, you twit.'

'Sorry, pal. It won't happen again. But what about you? You had a fall.'

'I'm not in the least hurt,' said Pat. 'Just a scratch on my nose. By the way, there's a stream nearby. Would you fancy a drink of cold mountain water?'

'I certainly would.'

Pat fetched the water in one of the plastic mugs and while Kitty drank it, she set a match to the firewood and watched the thin curl of blue smoke ascending upwards.

'I feel an awful ass for spoiling our day like this,' said Kitty. 'What time is it?'

Pat consulted her wrist-watch. 'Getting on for five.'

'We haven't much more than an hour and a half of daylight left. What if we have to spend the night here?'

'We'll be all right. We can snuggle together on the ground sheet with the rug over us, and I can stuff the haversacks with bracken for pillows. What could be more luxurious?'

Just as the sun was sinking they heard the sound of an engine.

'The helicopter!' exulted Pat, jumping to her feet and waving her arms in the air.

Kitty grabbed the red scarf and waved that as high as she could, screaming, 'We're here. We're here!'

The helicopter passed high over them and disappeared, and the girls felt despair in their hearts.

'Why couldn't they keep a proper look-out?' raged Pat. She slumped on the ground, the picture of gloom.

'Listen!' said Kitty. 'They're coming

back. Here, *you* wave the scarf.' She tossed it to Pat who sprang to her feet and began to wave frantically, at the same time jumping up and down, hoping the extra movement would attract the pilot's eye.

'They've spotted us,' said Kitty. 'Look, they're circling.'

Soon, the helicopter was hovering overhead. Pat hurriedly put out the fire and then a door in the helicopter opened and a rope ladder was let down.

'How on earth am I going to climb that?' asked Kitty.

Before Pat could reply, a pair of feet came into view and in two seconds, Dr. Ian Gregory was bending over Kitty.

'Ian! What are you doing here?' she asked, astonished.

'It's my job—search and rescue. Remember?'

'But you're in Australia.'

'Perhaps this is my ghost, h-mmm?' As he spoke he was examining her foot with a professional eye.

'Sprained or broken?' he asked Pat.

'Just a sprain, I think.'

'I'll leave that bandage on and put a support around it, and that should do until we get to hospital.'

Meanwhile, Richard and the co-pilot had descended from the 'copter with a stretcher, and Kitty was strapped into this and was soon in the plane.

'Where's Andy?' asked Kitty.

'He's taken my car,' said Richard. 'We didn't want to leave it here.'

'Of course not. I forgot about the car,' said Kitty.

The rope ladder was hauled in and the door shut. The engines revved and the plane took off.

Richard and Pat were sitting close together at one end of the cabin, while Ian sat beside the stretcher, holding Kitty's hand.

'Comfortable?' he asked, and when she nodded, he turned to Richard, and shouted above the noise of the plane,

'Congratulations, Richard.'

Richard looked at him in surprise. 'Thanks, but didn't you know we were engaged?'

'Of course. This is something else. The pilot told me that, just before he took off, he heard over the radio news that a Richard Willet had won five hundred dollars in a photographic competition. He recognised the name as being one of the people he was to pick up.'

'Whoopee! Five hundred bucks! Pat, we'll be able to get married right away.' They fell into each other's arms and stayed that way.

'Well, that's exciting news,' said Kitty. 'I'd almost forgotten about that competition. I guess Pat helped win it, too, just by being the model. Ian, you haven't told me about your father. How did you find him?'

'He's getting along nicely. I was able to catch a plane that landed me back here just before lunch, and I went on duty straight away.' He glanced at Pat and Richard, still embracing, and put his head close to Kitty's ear. 'We can't let those two have all the fun. How about it?'

'How about what?' Kitty leaned away and studied the face so close to hers.

' "How about what", she says. And they say a woman's intuition is sharper than a man's. Hasn't it dawned on you that I love you? I thought I'd shown it in so many ways.'

'Oh, Ian!' Kitty's face crumpled and, with a stupendous effort, she refrained from bursting into tears.

'How soon will you marry me?' Ian demanded.

'Just as soon as my ankle will let me hobble up the aisle,' whispered Kitty, her pain forgotten as ecstasy took over.

As Ian bent his head to kiss her, the pilot turned to tell them they would be landing in about twenty minutes.

'Holy Moses,' he said to the co-pilot. 'This crate isn't a rescue job any more.

It's a blooming love-nest.'

The co-pilot surveyed the scene and grinned.

'You're just jealous,' he said.

This Large Print Book for the Partially
sighted, who cannot read normal print, is
published under the auspices of

THE ULVERSCROFT FOUNDATION

THE ULVERSCROFT FOUNDATION

. . . we hope that you have enjoyed this
Large Print Book. Please think for a
moment about those people who have
worse eyesight problems than you . . . and
are unable to even read or enjoy Large
Print, without great difficulty.

You can help them by sending a donation,
large or small to:

**The Ulverscroft Foundation,
1, The Green, Bradgate Road,
Anstey, Leicestershire, LE7 7FU,
England.**

or request a copy of our brochure for
more details.

The Foundation will use all your help to
assist those people who are handicapped
by various sight problems and need
special attention.

Thank you very much for your help.